"Wo

"I really appreciate this. I realize we're taking advantage of you by keeping you away from your work. But don't worry, we'll make it worth your while."

That statement could be interpreted in more ways than one, Matt thought. "We'll have to start early," he told her. "Before daylight. Five o'clock."

"I'll be there," she said stoutly.

Matt doubted it. She looked more like a ten o'clock riser to him. "You could spend the night here," he suggested tentatively, curious to hear her reaction.

"Good idea." She sounded delighted. "That will save me a drive in the morning."

Not an instant's hesitation, he thought. She hadn't even paused to wonder if she'd have to fend off unwelcome advances if she accepted his invitation. That cheerful self-assurance made him want to shake her. Didn't she know that wicked dragons were always on the prowl for fairy-tale princesses? If she was looking on him as some kind of faithful old sheepdog who could be counted on never to present any problems, then maybe she had another think coming. He was feeling pretty dragonish himself.

Dear Reader,

Welcome to Silhouette—experience the magic of the wonderful world where two people fall in love. Meet heroines that will make you cheer for their happiness, and heroes (be they the boy next door or a handsome, mysterious stranger) who will win your heart. Silhouette Romance reflects the magic of love—sweeping you away with books that will make you laugh and cry, heartwarming, poignant stories that will move you time and time again.

In the coming months we're publishing romances by many of your all-time favorites, such as Diana Palmer, Brittany Young, Sondra Stanford and Annette Broadrick. Your response to these authors and our other Silhouette Romance authors has served as a touchstone for us, and we're pleased to bring you more books with Silhouette's distinctive medley of charm, wit and—above all—*romance*.

I hope you enjoy this book and the many stories to come. Experience the magic!

Sincerely,

Tara Hughes
Senior Editor
Silhouette Books

WYNN WILLIAMS

Starry Nights

Silhouette Romance

Published by Silhouette Books New York

America's Publisher of Contemporary Romance

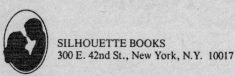

SILHOUETTE BOOKS
300 E. 42nd St., New York, N.Y. 10017

ISBN: 0-373-08649-0

First Silhouette Books printing May 1989

Printed in the U.S.A.

Canadian-born *WYNN WILLIAMS* has lived in the Pacific Northwest for most of her life. Her dream was to be an author, and now she travels with her engineer husband to research new locations for her Silhouette romances.

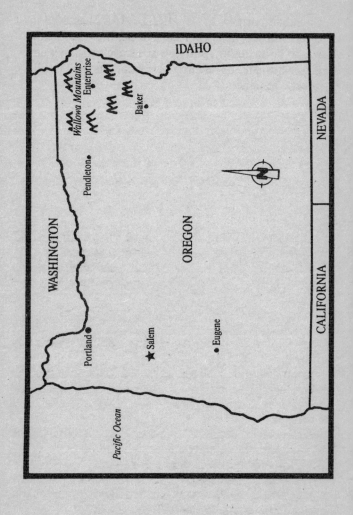

Chapter One

That's my offer!" Hob Skinner struck the table in front of him with the flat of his hand. "You better grab it."

Matt Kemper shook his head. "That's not an offer, that's an insult. At that price you'd be stealing the place, not buying it."

Hob pushed back his chair and got to his feet. "You can't hang on much longer, and you know it."

Matt looked up at the older man coolly. "That's my business."

"You better find a buyer before the bank snatches the whole ranch right out from under you. It's no secret that when your pa died he left you so deep in the hole you can't see daylight."

Matt's voice hardened. "Leave my father out of this. And don't forget your hat on your way out."

Hob slammed the front door behind him.

After a discreet interval, the ranch cook came out of the kitchen, wiping his hands on his flour-sack apron. "Hob Skinner's not staying for coffee?" he asked.

"Not this time, Willy." Matt stared out the window at the old truck speeding away from the house. "Did you hear what he said?"

"I was busy making doughnuts," Willy answered diplomatically.

"Hob talks loud enough for you to hear him in the next county." Matt ran a distracted hand through his thick fair hair. "I can't believe he hung on to enough of that money to make an offer for this place." He turned away from the window. "I'll be in the office. Adding up the bills."

Matt sat down at the scarred wooden desk and opened the big account book. He glanced up to see the old cook hovering in the doorway.

"Car coming up the road, boss."

"Hob coming back?" asked Matt.

Willy shook his head.

"Who is it, then?"

The cook shrugged. "None of my acquaintances drive little red sporty cars."

Matt slapped his pencil down on top of the unsatisfactory profit-and-loss figures for the past three months, thankful for any distraction from the prospect of financial disaster. "None of mine do, either, Willy. Maybe some tourist took a wrong turn."

"You want me to take care of it?"

"No, that's okay." Matt pushed back his chair and stood up, towering over the older man. "He'll make a change from all this red ink, whoever he is."

Matt walked from the office toward the front door, the sound of his booted feet sharp against the bare boards of the floor. The midmorning sun slanted brightly through the wide front windows. He paused a few feet from the curtainless glass to assess the visitor, squinting against the glare of light.

The jaunty little car trailed a plume of dust behind it as it sped up the gravel drive. It slowed abruptly and stopped almost a hundred yards from the house, the dust of its passage slowly settling while the occupant waited motionless in the driver's seat. At last, after what seemed to Matt to be a long pause, the car door opened and a young woman stepped out into the sunlight.

She stood with one hand resting on the roof of the car as she surveyed the house and its surroundings with careful deliberation, from Willy's straggling garden at one end to the stables and wooden corrals at the other. If she noticed Matt standing in the front window, she gave no sign.

"Looks like she's fixing to buy the place," said Willy, standing at Matt's elbow.

Matt gave him a look, and Willy returned to his kitchen. Matt went back to studying the young woman. She was small, slender and very slim waisted, but sweetly curved above and below, as her close-fitting shirt and jeans plainly attested. Matt realized that the two of them were dressed almost alike; he was also wearing Western boots, faded jeans and a blue work shirt with the sleeves rolled up. But only she was wearing a little red scarf—he would hardly call it a bandanna—tied at a jaunty angle around her slender throat.

His own clothes were faded by the strong sun of the eastern Oregon high country, well-worn by hard work and many washings, until the denim of his jeans was as soft and supple as chamois leather. Even from a distance he felt convinced that her clothes would look and feel exactly like his, only the manufacturer would have done all the work of making them that way. Designer labels and high price tags were what that kind of informal elegance was all about. He'd bet his last dollar that those jeans had never encountered a saddle, those boots never walked anything but concrete trails.

She reached into the car, pulled out an outsized leather bag and slung the strap over her shoulder before she started walking slowly toward the house. She looked to Matt like a little girl lugging a suitcase, or a fairy-tale princess whose wicked stepmother had set her tasks too big for her strength. Not that she was staggering under the load, he had to admit to himself. Not at all. As she came toward him, she carried the bag with an easy grace that belied its size.

Her hair was lighter than his, white blond, cut short in a froth of tousled curls that instinct told him had to be the work of an expensive hairdresser. Looking into the sun as he was, he couldn't make out her features. But he had the sudden conviction that her face would be beautiful. The exquisite perfection of the small slender body, the calm assurance of her bearing, promised that the reality could not be otherwise.

Everything about her was in miniature, but perfect. She reminded him of a small golden toy. She was—judging by the car she was driving—a toy that only a wealthy man could ever hope to possess.

He opened the door and went onto the porch as she mounted the low steps.

"Good morning," she said in a low, musical voice that sent a tingle up his spine. "I've been admiring your place, and I wonder if the owner would be interested in renting it for a short time."

His first lightning glance told him that her eyes were a deep, deep blue and that there were no rings on her slim tanned fingers. "I'm sorry, miss," he said. "This is a working ranch, not a dude ranch."

Her straight little nose was slightly shorter than he had pictured it and a little up-tilted. Her mouth was wider than he expected it to be, more mobile, more generous. And the blue eyes were sunnier. A faint sprinkling of golden freckles dusted her cheeks. But the clear, glowing skin, the cleanly molded bones of her face, the long, curling eyelashes, were all just as he had imagined them. As he stood looking down at her, he found himself estimating that the feathery arches of her eyebrows would come just to the pocket of his shirt.

"I'm Jillian Curtis," she said, unzipping the incongruously large bag and reaching into its capacious depths. "Here's my card."

He held the unexpected bit of pasteboard in his fingers without reading it, his eyes still on her face. "I'm Matt Kemper. Come in and have a cup of coffee," he said hopefully. "It's a long drive back to whatever city you came from."

Jillian followed him into the house. Excitement bubbled inside her as she looked around the sparsely furnished living room. Good furniture, what there was of it, heavy and masculine: leather couch, big chairs, an Indian rug on the far wall, antlers above the fireplace. Just like in the movies, she thought with an inward giggle, which she carefully concealed under her best business manner.

She perched on the front edge of the nearest chair. Its massive carved arms, capable of encircling a buffalo, seemed merely to tolerate her, as though she were something too small to be taken seriously. *That* was an attitude she was all too familiar with, and she didn't propose to put up with any such nonsense—from a chair or from its owner, who was now standing in the middle of the floor looking down at her, flicking her still unread business card against the thumbnail of his free hand.

Talk about fitting the part, she thought. Central casting could never have done better. One handsome young ranch owner in the flesh. Or perhaps she should say, on the hoof. In convincingly worn boots that added unnecessary inches to his already six-foot-plus height. On second thought, make that one *devastatingly* handsome young rancher. Not that his features were all that regular, now that she looked more closely. Still, there was definitely something about him . . .

She caught her racing thoughts, reminding herself that her interest was purely professional. For instance, it would be very interesting to see if a camera would catch that certain quality . . .

"So you're in the real estate business?" he asked.

"Real estate!"

The affronted note in her voice brought a puzzled expression to his face. "I didn't figure you were looking to rent this place for yourself. Or were you?"

"Well, no, as a matter of fact," she said in slight confusion. "Perhaps it would help if you'd read my card."

He glanced from the card to her and then back again. "So you're a production assistant?" he said mildly.

"That's right."

"Well, I'm sorry, Miss Curtis." His blue eyes were guileless, but the hint of a drawl in his voice broadened noticeably. "Living out here in the back country like this, I got to admit I don't have any idea what it is you produce. Or who you assist."

She felt her cheeks grow hot. But after a moment she looked at him frankly and smiled. "All right, I asked for that. Spare me the country bumpkin impersonations, and I'll try to explain what I'm doing here." She brushed her hair back with one slim tanned hand and took a deep breath. "I think maybe I'm just a little excited, now that I've seen your place. I'm scouting locations for a movie to be made in Oregon, here in this area. And this house, the corrals and barn, the lay of the land, it's—it's pretty close to what they have in mind." *Perfect* was what it was. *Exactly* according to specifications. But she didn't think it would be professional to rhapsodize over her wonderful astonishing find to the man who would be setting a price on it. Always providing, of course, that they would see it the same way back in Portland—and down in California. But of course they would. Unless they scrapped the whole project, this was where they would come.

He walked over to the fireplace and leaned against the heavy dark mantel.

If he had had on a Stetson, he would have shoved it up with the thumb of his free hand and tipped it to the back of

his head. The thought flashed unbidden into Jillian's mind,
and she blinked it out again. Just because he had the outward appearance of the ultimate movie cowboy, she mustn't
get him mixed up with the whole image. All that lean muscle and sun-bronzed skin might be deceptive, a facade
for... for a mean-minded disposition, or something even
worse. Maybe he's not a nice person at all, she told herself,
not believing it for a minute.

He said, "You work for a movie outfit that wants to make
a picture *here*?"

"I work for a film production company, an agency in
Portland. Andrea DiCicco is the head of it. Mostly we do
commercials. Local things. Some national political spots.
Television." She wondered if he believed her. His eyes told
her nothing. Intriguing, inscrutable, farseeing cowboy eyes.
Stop that, Jilly, she scolded herself silently.

"Yesterday Andrea got word that a Hollywood studio is
looking for a Western location—something different. And
they're thinking about the Wallowas. For the mountains and
the lake. And Enterprise and Joseph—"

She broke off as the swinging door to the kitchen was
pushed open and a small wizened man backed into the room
carrying a well-laden tray. The promised coffee was in a
surprisingly good china coffeepot. He placed the tray on the
round oak table, and Jillian seized the opportunity to
abandon the intimidating big chair. She slid into a straight
wooden one beside the table.

"Doughnuts!" she exclaimed. "Warm doughnuts. That's
the heavenly smell that's been tantalizing me since the moment I walked in. Did you actually make them yourself?"

The newcomer ducked his head and smiled at her wordlessly, then returned to the kitchen.

Since it seemed to be expected of her, Jillian poured the
coffee into two big willow-patterned cups that had the look
of family heirlooms. Matt crossed the room to sit opposite

her. She attacked the fragrant heap on the platter with the enthusiasm of a young person with a healthy appetite.

"You eat doughnuts?" he said, watching her.

Several quick retorts flashed into her mind, but she decided that it must be a rhetorical question and held her tongue.

In truth, his mental picture of her was sadly jolted. Fragile perfection and fat sugary doughnuts simply did not go together. He didn't exactly expect her to live on lettuce leaves and morning dew, he admitted to himself, but surely a girl like this would be used to something more rarefied. Caviar was the only food that came to his mind as being exotic enough to suit her. The imported kind, naturally. Or maybe she had champagne and pheasant waiting for her out in her expensive little red car and was just eating Willy's doughnuts to be democratic.

"So you're in the movies," he said.

The democratic one licked sugar off her fingers and said, "Oh, I'm not *talent*. I'm not in front of the camera. I'm production. That means that if it has to be fetched, I fetch it. If it has to be found or scrounged or begged or borrowed, I do that, too. Do you keep any chickens here?"

"Willy keeps a few out by the barn," he said. "Are we changing the subject?"

"Same subject," she said. "The script calls for live chickens. If they're on the premises, I won't have to raid anybody's hen coop some dark night. I don't suppose you have a hot air balloon handy, do you?"

"Sounds like it's going to be some strange movie," Matt said. "No, I'm fresh out of hot air balloons."

"Oh well, can't have everything." She gave him a brief mischievous smile that seemed to say that life was fun.

He admitted silently that the sunshine seemed a lot brighter than it had been just a short time ago, before the red car drove into the yard. He hoped that she wouldn't be too disappointed when she realized that the whole cockeyed scheme was simply impossible. He hated to have to break it to her that he was feeding her doughnuts under false pretenses, and they couldn't do business, after all. Not that the money wouldn't be welcome. A golden windfall was just what the place desperately needed.

Matt couldn't make himself believe for one minute that moviemakers were eager to pour money in his lap for the privilege of trekking two thousand miles away from their comfortable home base to run around his remote ranch with a bunch of chickens and a hot air balloon. It had to be a pipe dream. *She* believed it, that was obvious. And he didn't take pleasure in the thought of puncturing her illusions. He even wished they could come true. And not only for the money, but because it might keep her around longer.

"It's like this," he hedged. "The ranch—it won't run itself. I can't just turn it over to a pack of strangers and walk away for who knows how long. A week? A month? All summer?"

"But they'll pay you well. For every day they're here. I can't give you a time limit," she admitted. "I don't know enough about it. But everything about making a film is fantastically expensive—the cameras, the crews—everything. They won't waste a minute. They'll be in and out as fast as possible." Her blue eyes clouded a little. "Unless..."

"Unless what?" he prompted.

"Unless it turns out to be one of those epics where some wild-man director goes months over schedule and practically bankrupts the whole studio doing it." The clouds cleared, and Jillian added briskly, "But this sounds like a perfectly ordinary middle-budget production. With the middle of August as a tentative starting date. That would give you time to make any arrangements that are necessary. And I'm sure they won't be here for long."

Instead of giving her a direct answer, he said, "If they did come here, would you be coming with them?"

She sighed a little wistfully. "I'd love to, I really would. I've never been on a shoot for a full-length film. But that depends on what kind of deal Andrea can make with the studio. Andrea's good at hammering out deals, that's how come she's a producer. I'm good at details and organizing, but not so good at talking contracts and money."

Matt hated to take the shine off the day for her, but he couldn't escape the conviction that she was being wildly—totally—unrealistic. No one would ever make a movie in such an out-of-the-way corner as this. As gently as he could, he told her so.

His gentleness was wasted; Jillian's enthusiasm glowed even stronger as she explained to him why he was wrong. "They *want* to come. They *are* coming. It's just a matter of finding the right spot." She waved her hand toward the scene outside the window. "This spot." She looked around for her oversize bag, hopped up and brought it back to the table, where she spilled its contents beside her coffee cup to uncover a small camera.

"You don't mind it I take some pictures of this place, do you? Just the outside. I've already got a ton of shots of Enterprise, and the main street in Joseph, and the scenery between there and here."

He raised an inquiring eyebrow.

"Andrea got a call yesterday from one of her contacts in Los Angeles. So she packed me off to Enterprise, and I talked to some real estate people about properties in the area, and here I am. Mission completed. Or it will be, as soon as I get these pictures back to Enterprise. A pilot who's flying to Portland this afternoon will take them to Andrea so she can get them in the overnight mail to the studio."

"You *are* an organizer, all right," Matt said admiringly. He was amused at her breathless urgency over it all. You'd think that they were on the hot line to Moscow or something. He found it curiously touching that she could get excited over such starry-eyed foolishness.

"Now, then, if you'll kindly direct me to the railroad," Jillian said, "I can get a couple of shots of that before I start for home." She scooped everything but the camera back into the bag and stood up, ready to go back to work.

Frowning again, he got to his feet. "Railroad?"

"'One single-track railroad complete with steam locomotive.'" she quoted. "I was told in Enterprise that there is an old logging line not far from your place."

"Wait a minute. Slow down now. Is this railroad important to the movie?"

"An A1 priority," she said solemnly.

"Balloons and chickens won't satisfy them?"

"Definitely not. There has to be a locomotive for the chase scene."

"If that's the case, I think you'd better sit down again. And you can call off the airlift."

"You're saying that it's going to be a little difficult to get my locomotive?"

"*Difficult*, Jillian?" he said. "It's downright impossible." He realized belatedly that he had used her first name. "Not only that—you mustn't go up there. It could be dangerous to even try."

"How could it be dangerous?" Jillian demanded. He hesitated for a moment, and she studied him with a half frown. He certainly *looked* sincere. In fact, those strong cheekbones and the wide firm mouth seemed absolutely loaded with integrity. And there was something about him that she couldn't put her finger on—maybe it was the rough shagginess of his thick fair hair—that announced here was a fine young man who needed to be taken in hand by a well-organized young woman.

Whoa, Jilly, she told herself silently. The question is not whether he needs you to see he gets his hair cut, but whether he's about to distract you with some fairy tale intended to scuttle this movie project without putting the blame on himself.

"The railroad has been shut down, to start with," Matt said at last.

She maintained her steady gaze. "From April to August should give someone plenty of time to fire up one little locomotive."

"Charley Alcott is on the outs with the whole community," he said. "And the feeling is mutual."

"Charley Alcott?"

"Yes. The railroad belongs to his logging operation. He brings his logs down to the mill on flatcars. I don't suppose you remember, but last year we had a very dry summer. Now that engine is really old—"

"Really old! That's great—the older the better," Jillian broke in enthusiastically.

"And we had a couple of fires that started along the tracks," he continued, ignoring her interruption. "We finally realized that the old locomotive pouring out sparks was causing the trouble."

"Could it do that?"

"Charley didn't think so. He claimed that some troublemaker must be setting the fires to make it look that way. Now, that was crazy. There wouldn't be any point to someone doing a thing like that. It was Charley's locomotive, no mistake about it. Old Hob said it first, but the rest of us couldn't deny that when the train goes by and the fires spring up behind it, that makes pretty good circumstantial evidence. Some of the ranchers threatened to go to the law." Anger colored his voice, and she could see that last year's animosities had by no means died out.

"Feelings ran pretty high. Crop fires like that could put us out of business. I went up to try to get Charley's side of the story, but he just got madder. He jumped to the conclusion that I was accusing him, like everyone else. He said that he didn't have to prove anything to anybody, and I could take it or leave it."

"So you left it?" she said.

Matt shook his head a little ruefully. "I didn't have much choice. I was pretty hot under the collar myself by that time. And then one day Charley just shut down the whole works. Laid off the workers, put up No Trespassing signs all over the place. And that's the last we've seen of him."

"Where is he now?"

"Sitting up on the mountain, as far as anyone knows."

"So you don't think he'll say yes to renting us his railroad?"

"To having a bunch of Hollywood tenderfeet running around his mountain trying to make moving pictures? With a hot air balloon and a flock of chickens? What Charley will say isn't something a lady ought to hear."

"You don't know that for sure," Jillian protested.

"I know old Charley. I'd bet money on it."

She rummaged through her bag and found a notebook and ballpoint pen. "There must be some inducement that would make him change his mind. There's the money, for one thing." She wrote that down.

"Charley would rather be contrary than rich," Matt said.

"And there's the financial benefit to the whole area. Making a movie here could mean as much as a million dollars to the local economy."

He leaned over to watch her write in her notebook. "You better cross out that last part and hope that Charley doesn't get wind of it. He's not in the mood to do anything for the benefit of the community."

She looked past him, thinking hard. "I bet Andrea can get Senator Packwood to help, since the whole thing will bring so much money into the state. When local people get obstructive, a word to the top officials sometimes solves the problem."

"Except that in this case the top official *is* the problem," Matt reminded her. "It's Charley Alcott's rails and rolling stock. And he hates politicians."

"Maybe so. But if your senator calls from *Washington* and asks you to do this little thing..."

He shook his head slowly. "Charley's got no use for bureaucrats. Or Republicans. Or Democrats, for that matter."

Jillian's eyes narrowed. "You're certainly being negative."

"I'm just telling you how things stand."

"In that case," she said resolutely, "I guess it's up to me to take hold and get things done." She stood up.

Matt thought that she looked very small and gallant, summoning up her courage to go off and beard the lion in its den. Or was she merely the victim of mistaken self-confidence? Probably never met a man she couldn't wrap around her little finger....

"How do I get there?" she asked.

"I don't believe you can." He saw a sudden spark of anger in her blue eyes. He added quickly, "Not in that little red car, I mean. That road is mighty rough. And steep. You need a four-wheel drive."

"Well, I'll have to do the best I can." Her voice was cool. "So if you'll just give me the directions...?"

Matt got to his feet. "You can't go up there," he said, speaking slowly and distinctly, as though to a child.

Her chin lifted. "I *have* to get up there. It's my job." She slung the strap of the bag over her shoulder. "Thank you for the doughnuts, Mr. Kemper."

Just a few minutes ago they were well on their way to being on a first-name basis, Matt thought, and now they were back to "Mr. Kemper."

"Are you going to tell me how to find the way to the logging camp?" Jillian said. "Or do I have to find out somewhere else? I'd rather not go around asking directions and arousing unnecessary curiosity. But I'll do it if I have to."

"You're really bound and determined to have a look at that road, aren't you?"

"Not just to look at it. To travel up it to the end and see the locomotive."

"I'll drive you over there," Matt said abruptly. "Just to show you the road so you can see what you'd be up against. We'll go in my pickup."

"I appreciate your offer," she said carefully. "But it really isn't necessary. And I wouldn't want to inconvenience you."

"If you start off there in that little fancy car," he said with more heat than he intended, "I'll be spending the rest of my day hunting you up and towing you out of some pothole. So if you really don't want to cause me trouble, you'll get in my truck and let me drive you."

Her lips compressed. Matt could see that she wanted very much to refuse his ungracious offer. After a long moment's tussle with her pride, she nodded in silent assent.

Chapter Two

Jillian was quiet as she followed Matt down the front steps, the camera in her hand. As he went to bring the truck around, he looked back and saw her half-defiantly taking pictures of the house and other buildings.

She climbed in beside him without speaking. They rode in strained silence for a few miles, long enough so that Matt began to regret letting his temper get the best of him. After all, it wasn't her fault that she was lovely and expensive and accustomed to getting her own way.

He was searching for an amiable remark to bridge the gap between them when she spoke first.

"You're positive that Mr. Alcott is still angry?" she said thoughtfully. It sounded as though she wanted to be friends, too.

"I can't say what he is. I haven't seen him since Christmas. I don't know anybody who has."

"You mean that no one's talked to the man for months? He's up there all alone, and nobody even knows if he's alive or dead?"

"Now you're thinking of him as some poor old codger holed up on the mountain without a friend in the world," Matt said. "And it's not like that at all. Not that Charley's ever had too many friends, but there's a Mexican cook and a couple of old mossbacks who stay up there at the logging camp. The four of them likely spent the winter playing pinochle and spitting on the stove. And cussing out the rest of us. That's Charley's style."

"But you can't be sure of that."

"No, ma'am. Not without going up to see. Which Charley doesn't want anybody to do, or he wouldn't have spent his money for all these signs." He jerked his head in the direction of the No Trespassing sign on a fence post off to their left.

"It seems strange that he'd go into hiding like that," she said.

"I don't think he's hiding. I think he's just mad. Personally, I wouldn't be surprised if he has come down off his high horse long enough to actually ride his damn logging train. And when he saw all those sparks pouring down along the right-of-way, he knew that he was in the wrong. Naturally, he couldn't admit a thing like that, so he just shut down the operation. The timber business went to pot around that time, too, so he's not losing a whole lot of money by closing down for a while."

While Matt talked, they had been traveling on a good secondary road. Now he braked suddenly and turned off onto what was little more than a narrow track winding upward through the sagebrush toward the wooded slope of the mountain.

Jillian used both hands to steady herself against the lurching of the truck. "Is Charley Alcott a rich man?"

Matt shifted into a lower gear as the terrain grew steeper. "Charley Alcott's a lot like the rest of us," he said slowly. "Rich in land that doesn't happen to be producing a whole lot of dollars right at the moment. Some of us are just rich in mortgages. But they do say that Charley still has the first quarter he ever made. He's not up here living on squirrels and mice, if that's what you're thinking.''

The forest gradually began to move in closer. Pine trees crowded in, jostling them. Dark limbs reached out to touch the windshield, then scraped past the open windows and down the body of the truck.

The front wheels of the pickup lurched over an outcropping of bare rock and dropped with a jolt onto the soft forest floor just beyond.

Jillian pushed herself back from the dashboard with both hands. ''You were right,'' she said. ''This road is really terrible.''

''A road like this chews up little foreign cars and spits out the pieces,'' he agreed solemnly.

''Well, that scraping sound I just heard means that it can sink its teeth into big pickup trucks, too,'' she pointed out. ''Is there much more of this?''

''About eight miles. It's not all this rough, though. It should ease off a little past that bend up ahead.''

They rounded the curve he had indicated and found themselves in a wide grassy clearing, where for a short space the pine trees drew their dark skirts aside and let the midday sun shine in. At the far end of the glade, someone had cut down a pair of tall trees. The two fallen giants made a tangled barrier that effectively barred any further progress along the road.

Matt stopped the truck. Silence fell around them. ''No signs around telling us not to trespass this time. I reckon that Charley figured this says it plain enough.''

Jillian stared at the huge ponderosa pines that lay in their path. The wanton destruction left her speechless. One tree had been dropped squarely across the road, the other at a slight angle to rest on top of the first. Their tops entangled, the trees formed a barrier that was nearly head-high. A barrier as impenetrable as a brick wall.

The fact that there was a determined recluse living up there on the mountain became real to Jillian for the first time. This was a world very different from the one she was accustomed to, the world she moved in with confidence.

"How could he do a thing like this?" she said at last. "He must be crazy to destroy such big trees and block the road *forever*."

Matt kept his hands on the wheel as he turned to look at her. "A couple of men with chain saws could cut a path through there. Take them a few hours, maybe."

"They could?" She faced him expectantly.

He shook his head at her questioning gaze. "It wouldn't do any good. Not if Charley's serious about this thing. There'll be another roadblock farther on. Probably at the edge of a cliff somewhere. Charley was Mr. Nice Guy when he set this one up—he's left room for us to turn around. He wouldn't be that generous twice."

Jillian was not convinced. "If we can't get in, he can't get out. And that doesn't make sense. He *has* to come out sometime—if only to bring in supplies."

"Just about everything went in by the railroad when Charley was still running his train. Now I expect he's repaired some other old logging road, maybe one that comes out on the far side of the mountain. So he doesn't have to come this way anymore. That would explain why nobody's seen him lately." Her blue eyes still looked at him as though she expected him to do something about the situation, so he felt compelled to keep on explaining why nothing could be done. "If I were Charley, and still too stubborn to admit I was in the wrong, I'd go all the way to Baker or Pendleton to buy whatever I needed. I'd stay away from the people who might recognize me. And on the way home, I'd arrange a surprise or two for any uninvited company who found my new road. Like a bridge with loose planks I could take up after I was safely over it. Nobody would come driving up *my* mountain unless I wanted them to."

"He can't stay up there acting childish indefinitely," she said.

"Well, he can stay up there just as long as he feels like it. Or he can leave whenever he feels like it. Right this minute he could be in Las Vegas—or Australia. Nobody around here would know the difference."

Jillian studied Matt's set profile and decided he was serious. If the logging camp was deserted, she could get her pictures without having to make a lot of explanations. That would be a blessing. But it wouldn't be so handy for the negotiators if Charley Alcott was gone and no one knew where. Well, they'd worry about that problem when they came to it. Right now she had to tackle first things first.

She said, "Are you telling me that there's no way you could get up to that locomotive—even if you wanted to desperately?"

"Oh, I didn't say that," Matt answered innocently. "If I had any reason for seeing Charley Alcott—which I don't— I wouldn't let a little thing like a blocked road stop me. I'd just get myself a horse."

For a moment Jillian was speechless. What an obvious solution. "Of course!" she exclaimed. "That's the answer! And I bet you've got horses right there at the ranch, too!"

"Well, yes, I might lay my hands on one or two, if I put my mind to it." A trace of amusement escaped into his voice.

"Let's do it! Let's go back right now and get some horses!" In her enthusiasm Jillian reached out and clutched his forearm.

Her eyes widened and her thoughts derailed momentarily as she became suddenly aware of the reality of hard muscle beneath her fingers. For a moment of time the inside of the truck cab turned into a small charmed space where everything stood out in a sharper, clearer light. And the air was hard to breathe.

She snatched her hand back self-consciously, though his unguarded expression told her that he had felt the jolt, too.

Neither spoke for a moment. Then he blinked and shook his head slightly, as though to clear it. His face changed as he reached forward and restarted the engine. He shifted into reverse and looked over his shoulder at the way they had come. "I'll take you back to your car," he said flatly.

Puzzled, Jillian held her tongue. Matt wrestled the steering wheel as he jockeyed the pickup around roughly, grinding the gears as he shifted. As they started downward, he stepped on the gas.

Jillian braced herself again, feeling like a kernel of popcorn in a small overheated popper. "What's wrong?" she demanded.

" 'Let's go back and get some horses,' " he mimicked. "Can you even ride a horse?" he demanded harshly.

"Well, that depends." She wanted to say that of course she could ride, but she also wanted to answer honestly. "I think I'd be all right as long as it's a halfway civilized animal and not some bucking bronco. I may not be up to the local standard, but I'll probably be able to manage. Do we have to go so fast?"

He slowed the truck a little. "I thought you couldn't wait to get your pictures on that plane to Portland."

Now she had to stop and think. He was right about the snapshots. First priority had to go to getting them on their way. And she probably ought to talk to Andrea and let her know about the problem she had run into. Tell her that the rest of the pictures wouldn't be available for another day or so. . . .

Matt slowed the truck even further. "You're wasting your time." And mine, his tone implied. "You'd better find yourself some other place to play at the moving picture business. Another ranch. A different railroad. You're just heading for disappointment here."

She gave him a long level stare, but he continued to keep his eyes straight ahead.

"Is there another steam locomotive anywhere in the area?" She wouldn't ask him if there was also another ranch just like his own. She must be careful not to nudge him into taking a definite stand on renting his place. That might be disastrous when he was in this negative mood. Let him once give her a flat and final no, and masculine pride would never allow him to change it.

"No Hollywood people are going to come to this part of the country," Matt said. "They might talk about it and get everyone excited, but in the end you know they'll do what they always do—whatever's the cheapest. They'll make their movie in their own backyard."

Jillian had to bite back a sharp retort about his sudden insight into the film business. What had gotten into him, anyway? Just when they were getting along so nicely. Though *nicely* was hardly the word for it. *Sensationally* would be more like it, she thought with a little sigh as she remembered that brief touch, the spark that had passed between them. And right then the whole atmosphere had changed, barriers had come crashing down and the emotional temperature had dropped below zero.

She stole another glance at his set face, his hands clenched upon the steering wheel. He was definitely unhappy. And he had been just fine a few minutes before. B.T. Before Touching. The undeniable fact that he had responded to her physically had brought this on. There was one possible reason that she could think of for that. As always, she met the question head-on.

"Are you married?" she asked.

"What!" He took his eyes off the road to stare at her. The truck hit a chuckhole dead center, and the impact flung her against him.

She pushed herself back in a hurry. There was no point in making matters worse. "You know. Do you have a wife?"

"Good grief, *no*!"

"Engaged, then?"

" 'Engaged'?"

"You know. En—"

"Yes, I know what 'engaged' means." This quicksilver turn in the conversation seemed to baffle him. "And no, I don't have a fiancée."

"Well, then..." said Jillian carefully.

"Well, then *what*?"

"Then she won't object."

"She...?"

"Won't object to your driving me around like this. Though I do think if you had a wife she would have been thrilled at the idea of seeing her very own house in a movie."

"Her very own house...?"

"*And* her very own chickens."

Matt took a deep breath. "Something about talking to you can get a man dizzy." He relaxed a little and gave her a quick sidelong glance. After a moment he even smiled. "You know, if you're not careful, I might get the idea that all of this is an elaborate plot to sell me a hot air balloon."

"What?" Now it was her turn to be startled.

"Are you sure that's not what you're leading up to? You could peddle me a hot air balloon just so my nonexistent wife could see it featured in your nonexistent movie. Along with her ranch and Willy's chickens, of course."

"Oh." Now he sounded more natural. Jillian settled back in the seat, pleased with herself and the world in general. It just went to show that it never paid to beat around the bush. Somehow it didn't dampen her pleasure in the least to discover he was single, even though, now that she thought about it, a wife would have made a very strong ally in these circumstances. It just meant that she would have to rely on her own powers of persuasion. And once she had the pictures on their way and Charley's railroad in her pocket, then she would gladly turn her full attention to the fascinating problem sitting beside her. She caught sight of the paved road up ahead. Time to get down to business. Better not let her thoughts keep wandering down other byways, no matter how intriguing they might look.

"About the horses," she began carefully, choosing to start there rather than with the more potentially explosive question of whether he was willing to guide her.

"What about the horses?"

"Well, do you have any nice tame ones on hand? I haven't ridden since I was in my teens."

Matt gave her a quick glance. "That must have been all of a year and a half ago."

"You have to say that, or you wouldn't be gallant," she said serenely. "But I really am closer to thirty than I am to my teens."

Now they were back on the deserted highway, and he took the opportunity to subject her to a long searching stare. He took his foot off the gas and made it such a comprehensive appraisal that Jillian felt her cheeks grow warm.

"I've heard of women lying about their age, but this is ridiculous."

"It's the truth. I really am. Closer to thirty, I mean." She would be twenty-six in August.

"Sure you are." There was polite disbelief in his voice.

She made a move toward her bag and her driver's license, then pulled her hand back. She'd had to prove her age so many times that it was practically an automatic reflex. Just because she wasn't very big, everyone assumed she was still a little girl. Let him believe what he liked. How would he like it if he told everybody that *he* was—she squinted at him—about thirty-two, and then everybody said, "Oh, you can't be, you're just a kid." He'd hate it. But that would never happen to him, anyway, because he was tall and muscled and competent looking, instead of being a skinny little half-pint—

"Yes, I have quite a few," Matt said.

Jillian couldn't imagine what he was talking about. "Quite a few what?"

"Horses. Isn't that what we were discussing?"

"Oh. Well. That's great." Good heavens, whenever she had dealings with a man, he was usually the one who had trouble keeping his mind on the business at hand.

"But I can't guarantee that they'll be tame enough for you," he said.

"I'm sure they'll be just fine."

"You don't have the slightest idea of what you'd be letting yourself in for." His voice sounded severe again. "Getting up to Charley's won't be any Sunday canter around the park. Even if you can ride a horse, you're not going to waltz up the mountain for lunch and be back in time for dinner. You'd be lucky to get there at all."

"That's not what you said before," Jillian retorted quickly. "You said that you'd just get a horse and—"

"I didn't say *you* could do it!"

She bristled. "If a truck could go up that road, then a horse could surely go up there, too. And where the road is blocked, the horse just goes around the tree, or whatever, and gets back on the road and keeps on going. So where's the problem?"

"The problem is probably sitting up there at the logging camp playing pinochle. If I was in his boots, I'd figure I'd been nice and polite when I'd put down that first road-block—left plenty of room for unwelcome intruders to turn around and start back home. But there are some steep cliffs and hairpin turns between that spot and the logging camp. It wouldn't be any trick at all to fix things so *nothing* could use that track. At the very least, he could make it so that anyone who tried it—even on a horse—would have to detour around half the mountain."

Jillian was silent, thinking. "There *must* be another road," she said finally.

"Maybe. Over on the other side."

"With the planks out of the bridge, or something?"

"That's how I'd do it," Matt agreed.

She thought some more. "How about the railroad tracks? Couldn't horses follow them up to the camp?"

He shook his head. "Not if Charley didn't want them to."

"Don't you know anything but discouraging words?" she demanded.

"Sometimes 'home on the range' is different in real life than it is in the movies."

"Are you saying that you aren't going to rent me your horse?"

"A nice tame one?" he drawled.

"Are you being deliberately infuriating?"

"I'm never infuriating accidentally."

Jillian crossed her arms tightly and counted to ten. "I am coming back tomorrow," she said with slow precision. "And I am going to ride up that mountain."

"Nobody's going to be fool enough to rent you a horse and turn you loose on that trail by yourself," he said sharply.

"You're making it sound more impossible by the minute!"

"That's what I've been telling you from the beginning. It *is* impossible."

She contradicted him sturdily. "That's not what you said before." Growing up with four strapping older brothers had taught Jillian that a girl could never let masculine arrogance pass unchallenged. Not if she wanted to call her life her own. "You said that you could get up there if you wanted to."

"That's different." His voice was flat.

"It doesn't have to be." Jillian modified her tone to sound more businesslike. "You can rent me one of your horses— and your services as a guide. Just for a quick trip up there and back. And DiCicco Productions will pay whatever you ask," she added recklessly.

"I'm sorry. I can't do that," he said with complete finality. "You go on back to Enterprise. Take care of your snapshots. Talk to some of the townspeople—they'll tell you the same thing I have."

She heard that note of finality with a sudden stab of alarm. Teasing, challenge, even anger, she could deal with. This was different. She felt she had given a brief glimpse of hidden depths, unsuspected worlds that she knew nothing about.

The approach to the ranch house was just ahead. As the truck turned off the highway, Jillian had a sense of time running out.

"I don't think it's a good idea for me to talk to anyone else about this," she said slowly, breaking the constrained silence that had fallen between them. "You're the only person I've told that there may be a movie shot here."

He nodded. "I guess that's right. Don't get the natives all stirred up over nothing." After a pause, he said, "How did you happen to find your way to my place, then?"

"I talked to a real estate man in Enterprise. I didn't say I wanted to *buy* a ranch, just that I was interested in one with a certain kind of house—and he mentioned that it sounded like the Kemper place. After that, I didn't ask him any more questions, not even how to get here. I got a gas station attendant to give me directions."

"I see," he said noncommittally. "That was pretty clever of you."

They pulled into the front yard, and he stopped the hard-worn pickup parallel to her bright red sports car, giving the smaller vehicle a good eight feet of clearance. "I'd hate myself if I put a scratch on that expensive paint job," he said, opening the door and swinging himself out of the truck in one continuous fluid motion.

"Me, too," she agreed wholeheartedly. She tugged her heavy bag out with her, carried it over and dropped it onto the passenger's seat of the Porsche. She turned to face him, then realized that there was nothing to do but say her good-byes and be on her way.

Jillian was aware of Matt's eyes on her as she started the engine and put the car in gear. Even when she eased up on the clutch and the wheels began to turn, she hoped that he would call her back, tell her he had changed his mind. She drove down the road slowly, keeping his tall figure in her rearview mirror. He stood motionless, not even turning when the old ranch cook came out of the house to stand at his side.

"Pretty," said Willy, not specifying whether he meant the car or the girl.

"You have any idea how much a car like that costs?" There was anger in Matt's voice. He went on without waiting for an answer. "A fortune. Thirty thousand dollars, at least. Maybe more."

"She coming back?"

"It'll be better if she doesn't. There's nothing here that could possibly interest a girl like that."

"I suppose she's got a sugar daddy," Willy said inelegantly.

Matt's memory of those sunny blue eyes made it hard to accept the idea of a generous lover. "She's filthy rich, Willy. Either she was born that way, or she's got a job that's coining money hand over fist. Whichever it is, she's out of our league." He shook his head reflectively. "I've known girls like that before. One in particular...." For a moment he was no longer looking down the road, but back into the past, remembering other blue eyes and chestnut hair instead of blond. "I learned that when it comes right down to the crunch, those girls always go where the money is. I guess you can't blame them too much."

Willy spat in the dust. "I never cared for little cars like that. They make you feel like you're scooting along sitting on the pavement. Give me a pickup anytime. I like to see where I'm going."

STARRY NIGHTS   35

"Me, too, Willy," said Matt. But as he turned away from
the empty road, he remembered the ledgers on the desk, and
the thought came unbidden that the one thing in the world
he could no longer do was see where he was going.

Chapter Three

Jillian drove to Enterprise slowly, oblivious to the power under the red car's hood. Her mind was busy with the problems ahead of her. And behind her. How much easier things would be right now if only Matt Kemper had agreed to guide her up to that logging camp. That was obviously the best solution to her present difficulty. But the finality in his voice when he said, "Sorry, I can't do that," had left her no room for argument, logical or otherwise.

That finality had been like a closed door, shutting her out. It was a rejection all the harder to accept after those moments of rapport they had experienced together, moments that had sparked between them as bright and fleeting as a tiny shower of fireworks.

Forget that, Jilly, she told herself sternly. Time to get her mind back on her job. Somehow she had to figure out how she was going to organize an expedition up into these mountains that surrounded her, starting from a town where she was a stranger—and do it all without publicizing the reason behind the trip.

She forced herself to organize her thoughts. First, she should call Andrea at the office and let her know about these latest developments. Second, label the snapshots and get them on their way. And why hadn't Matt asked if *she* happened to be engaged, when he'd had such a perfect opportunity? She knew, from listening to her brothers, that most men automatically checked a woman's left hand for rings on first meeting, to get an idea of her availability.

But the absence of an engagement ring didn't necessarily prove a thing. She could easily imagine several scenarios that would account for that. For instance, she could be about to marry some young scientific genius who was devoted to her but too dedicated to medical research to squander his meager salary on diamonds. And she wouldn't want him to do that, of course. Or, for all Matt Kemper knew, there could be a millionaire jet-setter waiting for her this very minute with an umpteen-carat diamond ring he'd had designed especially for her third finger, left hand.

The vivid fantasy faded. What was she doing? Driving along mooning like some giddy schoolgirl, that's what she was doing. Matt Kemper hadn't been interested enough to ask. That was that. It was time she got her mind back on the job she had come for.

Jillian parked the Porsche in front of the low wooden rail fence that separated the weed-filled parking area of the Enterprise airport from the narrow airstrip itself. She sat in the front seat while she labeled the individual snapshots and collected them into a brown manila envelope with "DiCicco Productions" printed on the front. She stuffed a handful of pictures that were too blurry to be worth sending back into her bag.

The airport terminal was a large brown wooden hangar with a very small space partitioned off one front corner for an office. Jillian went inside to tell the pilot everything was ready. While he went out to make his preflight check, she used her telephone credit card to place a call to Andrea in

Portland. Jillian stood beside the window with the receiver to her ear as she waited for the connection to be made.

When Andrea came on the line, Jillian started speaking without any preliminaries beyond identifying herself. Andrea hated for people to waste her time.

"I think I've found exactly what we are looking for," she said crisply. "There's a ranch not too far out of town that will be perfect. And I'm pretty sure the owner will be agreeable about renting it. Now, about the—"

"What do you mean, 'the owner will be agreeable'?" Andrea cut in. "You didn't tell him what this is all about, did you? The last thing Bernie wants is to have the word get out before they've even *seen* the place. I thought you understood that, Jillian."

"Listen, Andrea, what they'd like and what is possible may be two different things," Jillian replied. Her cardinal rule was that she didn't let anyone bully her. Not her brothers, not her boyfriends and not her boss, either. "I've discovered that around here you can't just go snapping pictures on somebody's property without being ready to tell him what you're up to."

"Well, I would have expected you to have had more sense than to tell him the truth."

Jillian remembered her own bubbling excitement at the first sight of the Kemper ranch. And of Matt. Had she talked a little too freely? Perhaps she should have made up some plausible falsehood on the spot. No, she decided, it would have been stupid of her to try. Lying was not one of her talents. She said, "I'd just driven half a mile up his private road in this car of yours that's as conspicuous as a circus parade, and I'm standing there with my camera in my hand. What am I supposed to say—that I've come to immortalize the place on film for *National Geographic*?"

Anyway, she was positive that he could be trusted to keep her secret. "The owner won't breathe a word to anyone," she assured Andrea.

"Well, maybe not—if you batted your eyelashes at him."
Andrea sounded calmer now.

Jillian gritted her teeth to suppress a stinging retort. Andrea wasn't the only one who believed that Jillian accomplished what she did mainly because other people—namely men—went out of their way to coddle her. Andrea was just the only one who made a habit of mentioning it. Andrea herself was five foot nine, brunette, broad shouldered and forceful. A combination that Jillian secretly considered quite enviable. At least no one looked at Andrea and automatically assumed that she needed a big strong man to pat her on the head and tell her what to do.

"I've run into a much bigger problem than that," she said. "You remember that I told you last night I'd heard about a locomotive that seemed just perfect? Well, it looks like there are going to be complications." She told Andrea about her abortive trip to Charley Alcott's logging camp.

Andrea was blunt. "Well, the whole thing sounds ridiculous. There has to be another road up there somewhere."

"If there is, then Matt Kemper doesn't know about it. And if I find it, it will probably have some kind of roadblock, too."

"I'm running up a lot of expenses on this gamble, Jillian. Pictures of that locomotive are essential. They may be the one thing to swing the deal. The job's only half-done without them." She paused to think. "I'll be at the Portland airport to meet the chartered plane, so I can get this first set of pictures off to Los Angeles by overnight mail, but I've got to be able to tell Bernie that the rest are on their way."

Jillian waited as Andrea went on thinking aloud, sounding uncharacteristically distracted. "I wonder, maybe you ought to fly back with the pictures. Then you'd be on hand when Bernie calls to ask questions—I know he's going to call as soon as he sees them, if they're as good as you say they are. But then you'd have to get back to Enterprise. And, of course, you'd have to leave the Porsche. I certainly wish I had my car here, Jillian."

"So do I." Jillian spoke with feeling. She had listened to Andrea's speech with mixed emotions. The chance for a person-to-person conversation with an actual Hollywood producer hadn't come her way so far in her career. It was an opportunity she hated to miss. On the other hand, she'd hardly like him to remember Jillian Curtis as the person who only got half the job done. It was a moot question, anyway. Andrea was never going to let her fly back and leave the Porsche behind, all by itself in a strange town. That car had been Andrea's share of a divorce settlement, and as far as Jillian could tell, she cared more for it than she had for her departed spouse. Andrea used it as an advertisement for DiCicco Productions. A "see how successful we are" sort of thing. Nothing but the prospect of doing business as part of a full-blown Hollywood production would have compelled her to part with it, even temporarily.

"If only that little van of yours was more dependable," Andrea said reproachfully. Obviously she was still regretting her sudden impulse to dispatch Jillian to Enterprise in the speediest vehicle available.

"Well, it just isn't," Jillian said stoutly. "It's getting old, and it doesn't go anywhere in a hurry anymore. But I wish I did have it here—it might be a little less conspicuous than the Porsche. Or maybe not. What I need to blend in around this place is a pickup truck. A middle-aged one. Maybe with a bale of hay in the back."

"Well, try to keep the expenses down," Andrea said. "Do what you have to do to get up to that locomotive. Don't waste any time. Be sure to call me tomorrow with a progress report. And tell that pilot of yours to get here before three o'clock this afternoon." She hung up.

Jillian put down the receiver and stared, unseeing, out the window for a few minutes, her mind working furiously. There seemed to be no logical good place to begin. This wasn't something she could arrange on her own. To get what she needed, she was going to have to ask for help. And ask it from the right person.

The lanky middle-aged pilot had finished inspecting his plane and had turned to look expectantly in her direction. Jillian gathered up her bag and the brown envelope. Might as well start her questioning with the person nearest at hand, she thought. At least the pilot would be out of town the rest of the day and wouldn't be around to help the rumors get started.

She handed over the pictures and relayed Andrea's instructions. "Is there someplace around here I could rent a horse?" she asked, trying to make it sound like an afterthought.

His glance flickered from her to the bright sporty car waiting at the edge of the field. "You want a horse?"

Jillian could almost see the questions forming in his mind. She offered him the only explanation she had been able to think of while standing there looking out the window. "I've been here a couple of days, touring around, looking at the countryside. And I wondered if there was any way of taking a ride up into the mountains."

He looked down at her thoughtfully. "A trail ride, you mean?"

She nodded.

"They do quite a bit with day trips out of Joseph, up around the lake," he said.

That wasn't the direction she wanted to go. "I was thinking maybe over that way," she said, motioning vaguely northward.

His glance sharpened. Jillian tried to look guileless, knowing that his was just the first of many such glances she might have to meet if she was going to see this through without giving the game away.

"Well," he said slowly, "there're a couple of fellows around town who take dudes on pack trips, if that's what you had in mind. I don't know if they're available right now. Or if they make a practice of traveling over *that* way." He mimicked her sketchy gesture.

Jillian thought she heard suspicion in his voice. He probably thinks I'm searching for lost gold mines, she told herself a little desperately. Would that be better or worse than the actual truth? She had a sudden vision of half the population of Enterprise and Joseph streaming after her carrying picks and shovels.

"My advice would be to try over at Pete Risling's place," the pilot said. "He could be out of town, but his wife or one of his boys should be able to steer you to the right outfit."

This was getting more impossible by the minute, Jillian thought.

"Or if worse comes to worse," he went on, "I suppose Hob Skinner might take you."

"Hob Skinner?" she asked hopefully. At least he would be only one person to explain to, and not half a dozen.

"Hob's mostly available. He's not exactly a guide. Or anything else in particular. But he could probably put together some kind of pack outfit if you made it worth his while. Depends on how bad you're wanting to go, I guess."

Jillian glanced away. "Oh, I don't know," she said. "It sounds more complicated than I expected. Maybe it's not worth the bother."

She watched as the plane took off, and then walked slowly back to the car. It was beginning to look as though she could either get up to see Charley Alcott's locomotive, or she could keep her secret. Right now she didn't see how she could do both.

She drove into the center of Enterprise, stopped at a small café for a hamburger lunch and tried to formulate a plan of action while she ate. The pilot had sounded dubious about Mr. Skinner. But somehow he seemed easier to approach than Mr. Risling, with his wife and large family. Easier to fool, she corrected herself grimly. Easier to lie to. Except that lying never did come easy to her. And this one would have to be a whopper. She finished her meal without tasting it and without coming up with a workable idea.

Face it, she told herself, there is no believable excuse in the world for you to go riding up to that particular spot. There isn't even an unbelievable one. Such as, she had a tip that there was a pot of gold buried under the locomotive? Or Bigfoot was nesting in the caboose?

No, forget all that. She had to be going up there to see Charley Alcott. She didn't have to hide that fact, just the reason behind it. She could look someone straight in the eye and say, "I have to go up in the hills and talk to Charley Alcott. Will you take me?" That shouldn't be so hard.

At least not until the other person looked *her* straight in the eye and asked, "Why?"

Then what would she say? That she'd just learned he was her long-lost uncle? Or he'd been remembered in somebody's will and she was delivering the check? No, she wasn't actress enough to carry off that kind of story and make it convincing. But the mental picture of a check in an envelope in her purse suddenly triggered another idea. Perhaps she could simply look distressed and say something like, "I have a letter to deliver—I simply have to get up there! Please help me!"

If they pressed her for more details, she could tell them that it was personal. Let them imagine whatever they liked, as long as they didn't guess that someone was thinking of making a movie in the area.

It wasn't even really dishonest. She certainly had letters in her well-stuffed bag. And she certainly needed to see Charley Alcott. Well, not precisely. It was his locomotive she had to see. Someone else would be dealing with Mr. Alcott later on. But at least it was a plan! Something that she could do. It could even work.

Jillian gathered up her things with enthusiasm. Now for a public telephone and the local directory. She hesitated be-

tween the well-recommended Mr. Risling and the more
doubtful Mr. Skinner, before settling on the latter. She
would feel more confident in putting on her little charade
for a single set of masculine eyes. A family group might be
harder to fool. And there had been no mention of a Mrs.
Skinner.

Hob Skinner lived on the very fringe of town, at the tail
end of an obscure street. Jillian had to stop and inquire at a
gas station—taking care not to use the same one at which
she had received directions to the Kemper ranch—before she
could find the house.

Her first impulse was to drive on, but she made herself
turn into the driveway and stop the engine. The house was
small and run-down, the porch sagging. Beyond it, on what
Jillian guessed to be maybe a half acre of land, there were
some barren plots of ground, empty pens fenced with torn
chicken wire and several sheds in various stages of decay.
Nothing moved. She heard no clucks, no squawks, no animal sounds at all. The sweet spring day was glumly silent
here, and the air seemed to smell dustily of failure.

Jillian couldn't imagine what kind of small animals had
eked out their existence in those ragged pens. And surely no
horses lived in the collapsing sheds. Hob Skinner must have
gone out of the trail guide business. Judging by his surroundings, that wouldn't be the first business he had gone
out of. She leaned forward and turned the key in the engine.

The front door of the house opened. A stringy weather-
beaten man in faded work clothes came down the broken
steps, quickening his gait as he approached the car. He put
his hand firmly on the door handle, effectively thwarting her
intention to leave. She guessed him to be in his mid-fifties.
He was thin faced and sharp eyed, clean looking except for
a two-day stubble of beard.

He bent down to bring his head to the level of the car
window and give her what he apparently intended as a wel-

coming smile. "Well, well, this is a surprise, seeing you again so soon."

Jillian was too taken aback to answer for a moment. She said, "You must be mistaken. I don't think—"

"Saw you this morning," he said. "Driving around outside town. What are you doing—taking the census?"

"No, I'm not. I'm not a census taker—"

"Course you aren't. Not in an expensive car like this." He pulled the door open. "Come on in. I'll make coffee."

"Thanks just the same," she said hesitantly, "but I don't want to bother you, Mr. Skinner."

His almost colorless gray eyes had been greedily taking in the details of the car interior. Now they flicked back to her face and were still. Jillian could have bitten her tongue. Revealing that she knew his name was a definite mistake. It spoiled any chance she might have had of playing a lost traveler looking for instructions back to the main road.

"Come in," he repeated, holding the door wide. "It won't be no bother."

Reluctantly, Jillian turned the engine off. Short of backing out of the yard with him hanging on to the door handle, she didn't seem to have a choice.

The inside of the house wasn't as bad as she had expected, though the heavy old furniture was drab and dull. Nice enough, once, but worn now. She sat on the edge of a straight wooden chair and put her bag at her feet.

Hob Skinner went into the kitchen and came back again almost at once, as though he was afraid she might slip away if his back was turned too long. He handed her a thick pottery mug of rather scummy-looking coffee.

"City girls don't use milk or sugar," he said positively. "I know that." He sat in a chair opposite her and looked at her expectantly. "What city you come from? Boise? Salt Lake? No, that's not right. Oregon license on the car, wasn't it? Portland, maybe?"

Jillian nodded slowly, gathering her wits. She might not be much of a performer herself, but she had seen a lot of acts and acting, and it seemed to her that his garrulous-old-codger routine was just a shade too broad. She didn't sense any physical menace from the older man, but there was a tension in his shoulders, a fixity to his gaze, that spoke of some inner pressure he was trying to conceal.

"So you're all the way from Portland," he went on. "You here on business?"

Playing for time, Jillian sipped from the heavy mug. It tasted like instant coffee made with lukewarm water. "I've been driving around the area for a couple of days," she said blandly. "Just looking around, you know."

He stared at her.

"And you come to just look around my place, too?" he asked.

"Oh, there seems to be some kind of misunderstanding," she said carefully. "I was thinking I might do some horseback riding while I'm here—a city girl in the wide-open spaces, you know. We do get these romantic ideas." She gave him one of her best smiles.

He didn't seem to notice. "So why did you come here to me?"

"Oh, somebody mentioned your name," she tossed off airily.

"My name? Who mentioned my name?"

Think fast, Jilly, she told herself. Drink some more of this vile liquid. She was still holding the cup, because there was no place handy to set it down. This man looked entirely capable of hunting down that pilot to cross-examine him, capable of rousing the whole town's curiosity.

"I didn't ask him his name," she said, truthfully enough. She'd already known it at the time, there was no need to ask.

"What does he look like, then?" he persisted.

Jillian fluttered her eyelashes at him. Andrea would have been proud of her. Hob Skinner didn't seem impressed. He just waited for the answer to his question.

"You probably don't even know each other," she parried. "He thought you were in the trail-guiding business, so he must have you mixed up with somebody else."

Hob Skinner frowned. "I can put together a trail outfit—if it's worth my while," he said slowly. "Is that what you're here for?"

"Me? Heavens no!" She wouldn't hire Hob Skinner as her guide if it meant she never got there. "I've hardly been on a horse for years."

Hob Skinner gave no sign of having heard this disclaimer. "Is a trail guide what you were looking for out at the Kemper place?"

"What?" The question caught her unawares. Her first impulse was to deny it completely, to tell him that he must be mistaken.

"I saw you driving in there this morning as I was driving out," he said before she could formulate a denial. "Couldn't mistake that car, not another one like it around here."

"Oh." Jillian vaguely recalled a pickup truck passing her as she turned off the highway onto the road to the ranch house. "I've been doing such a lot of sight-seeing," she responded casually. "Which ranch is the Kemper place?"

Hob Skinner was silent, studying her. "You in the real estate business?" he asked finally.

Jillian shook her head in genuine annoyance. What was it about her that made people conclude she must be selling real estate? "No, I am not!" she said with emphasis.

"Because if you are—" the pale eyes flickered momentarily, then settled on her face again "—then you're wasting your time talking to Matt Kemper."

"I don't believe that what I do with my time is any of your business, Mr. Skinner." She was coldly angry now. "I'll talk to anyone I please."

"Kemper ranch business will be *my* business pretty soon," he said. "Best you should remember that."

Jillian had moved forward slightly on her chair, preparing to stand up and get out, but his last words made her pause. "I don't understand," she said.

"Matt Kemper's been running that place straight into the ground ever since he took over from his pa. It used to be one of the best spreads in the valley, until Matt got hold of it."

"That's hard to believe." She spoke coldly, not wanting to hear any more of this scurrilous talk about Matt. But curiosity mixed with dread kept her from moving.

Hob Skinner seemed to sense that he had trapped her into paying attention. "That Matt," he began, while Jillian tried to hold her face rigidly expressionless, "I don't know what's wrong with that boy. I'm not saying anything against old Jim Kemper and his missus, but it seems like there must be bad blood there somewhere for a youngster to turn out like that."

Jillian compressed her lips together tightly. She wasn't about to give him the satisfaction of asking a single question. But Hob Skinner was in full spate now. He needed no encouragement.

"If a man can't make money, he could at least make a few friends. But Matt Kemper can't do that, either. Can't keep the ones he started out with. Even turned against his own blood relatives."

Suddenly the sad little house seemed drearier than ever to Jillian, the atmosphere more oppressive, as though a cloud had passed over the sun. How much of this condemnation was the truth, and how much was just a disgruntled man's spite?

"It's not as if he had enough kin he could cut off a few without making any difference. Matt's the only Kemper left.

And there's not many of his ma's folks around, either. They don't have anything to do with Matt, though—not since the trouble."

He paused expectantly. Jillian was unable to hold back the question. "What trouble?" she asked.

"Nothing to worry your head about, not now—not if it's the *property* that you're interested in," he said slyly. "Matt's real problem with the ranch is that he could never take a nickel out because he never put a nickel in. The beef business takes capital these days. You can fix fence and herd your stock around all you want, but sweat don't take the place of money."

"All this has nothing to do with me."

"Maybe not. But just so you don't get the wrong idea— it ain't going to be Matt Kemper's place much longer," he said. "Anybody that's interested in that ranch is going to be dealing with me. Anybody thinking of buying should know that it's in a lot worse shape than it looks. It'll take a heap of capital to undo all the years Matt's been dragging it down."

Jillian looked at Hob Skinner with cold distrust. Why was this peculiar man telling her all these things? Why this sudden outpouring of information to a perfect stranger? Information that her instincts told her had to be at least biased, if not flatly untrue.

She allowed her disbelief to show. "You seem to be saying that the Kemper ranch isn't worth having. And at the same time, you expect me to believe that you are in the process of buying it yourself. And that you can provide the operating capital you say it needs. I'm afraid I can hardly accept any of those statements."

She swept the shabby room with a disdainful glance before turning to look pointedly out of a dusty window at the evidence of failed enterprise that littered the land surrounding the house.

"But this here's a rented house, not my own place," Hob
Skinner said indignantly. "You can't expect a man to waste
good capital on no-account property like this. All that out
there—that was more like hobbies, you might say."

Jillian was interested only in getting away from this place.
"Mr. Skinner, this entire conversation has been a mistake."

"No, I don't think so." His voice was confident. "A city
woman in a rich fancy car drives into Matt Kemper's ranch
this morning and then shows up at my place this afternoon." He said it as though it proved something. "Two and
two makes four, every time."

"Well, I'm afraid that you have made a hundred and four
out of it in this instance, Mr. Skinner. I assure you that I am
in no way involved in buying property, any property at—"

"That's all right with me," he interrupted, oozing the
same maddening self-assurance. "I'm not expecting you to
lay your cards on the table—not at this stage of the game.
But I wanted you to know just how things stand. Now you
can take it from here."

The only thing she was going to take from here was herself, Jillian thought, and she was going to do that as quickly
as possible. She stood up. "I have to be going. Thank you
for the coffee." She looked around to find a spot to leave the
nearly full cup.

Hob Skinner got to his feet. Jillian turned away from him
to place the cup on a small gateleg table that stood against
the wall. She sensed his movement, but she couldn't see
what he was doing behind her. She heard her heavy bag
topple onto its side and turned back to see her camera and
some of her other belongings go sliding out onto the worn
linoleum. What she saw next was Hob Skinner's bony fingers scrabbling to scoop up her photographs and bits of paper off the floor.

"There, I think I got them," he said, straightening up with his hands full of the snapshots she had decided not to send Andrea.

Jillian put her hand out in a commanding gesture, but he made her wait, in an agony of impatience, while he shuffled through the bunch, scrutinizing each one carefully before he handed it over. She couldn't remember whether there had been any pictures of the Kemper ranch among the duds. She could just imagine what he would make of it if there were.

Hob Skinner shook his head over the quality of her photography as he dealt them one by one into her waiting hand. "Looks like you ought to get yourself a different camera," he said. "Maybe one with a special lens for taking pictures of mountains." He studied the pictures of the town longer than the landscapes. "This here blurry one looks like the Wilderness Inn. I suppose that's where you're staying."

She pretended not to hear the questioning note in his voice. The less he knew about her, the better it would be. This whole encounter had turned into a disaster. There was only one positive thing she could find to say about it. By some lucky fluke, she hadn't given him her name.

After maddening deliberation, he surrendered the last of the snapshots. Jillian saw, to her overwhelming relief, that it was just as innocuous as the others. For the first time she detected a hint of uncertainty in Hob Skinner's pale eyes. They had turned out to be such innocent, touristy-looking pictures. Perhaps he was wondering if she could be just what she claimed—a city girl taking a few days to drive around the countryside. For a moment she dared to hope that she had navigated through these tricky rapids and come out unscathed on the other side.

Then she saw that he had held something back. He had a piece of white pasteboard in his hand.

"Nice-looking business card you carry around with you."
Slyly triumphant, he looked from the card to her face and
back again. "What's DiCicco Productions?" he asked.

Chapter Four

Sudden anger, as swift and hot as a lightning bolt, flashed through Jillian's body. Rashly, unthinkingly, she stepped forward. Her free hand darted out in an attempt to snatch away the telltale card.

Hob Skinner pulled back and turned his body sideways to keep the card easily out of her reach. "What's a production assistant?" he demanded.

Jillian stared at him wordlessly, bringing the blaze of her anger under firm control before she spoke. "You have no business taking things from my bag," she said slowly and distinctly.

"Why, I only picked up what you spilled." His voice was self-righteous. "And I just gave you everything back, right there in your hand. Except for this little business card. People go around all the time giving these things away."

"Well, I didn't give it to *you*, so you can just hand it right back."

He looked at her, then at the card. He shook his head. "I think I'll keep it." He tucked it carefully into the pocket of his faded shirt.

Jillian bit back more angry words. The damage was done now. Demands and shouting would only make it worse. She should have been clever enough to react with indifference, as though his find was of no importance. And hope that he would assume the card had no connection with what she was doing here. But it was too late for that now.

She reached down to retrieve the fallen camera, thinking furiously as she stuffed it back into her bag along with the snapshots. She was wondering if Hob Skinner was going to canvas the town, buttonholing everyone in sight, in an effort to ferret out more information about her. She wouldn't put it past him. But he wasn't apt to get any satisfaction that way, because no one around here knew anything to tell him. The pilot from the airport knew that *something* was going on, or there wouldn't have been that hurry-up flight to Portland. But he wouldn't be back in Enterprise until tomorrow. And maybe, with any luck, she would be gone by then.

She gave Hob Skinner a brief parting glance, as cool and self-assured as she could make it. "Goodbye, Mr. Skinner," she said. "Your hospitality leaves a great deal to be desired."

Driving away, Jillian tried to tell herself that it could have been worse. He could show the card and ask his questions, but DiCicco Productions would be a complete mystery to everyone for three hundred miles around. Everyone except Matt Kemper, she remembered with a start. He knew the whole story. But he wouldn't tell Hob Skinner what he knew. Of course he wouldn't. And Hob Skinner wouldn't ask him, anyway. Not after the naked hostility he'd expressed toward Matt. And yet . . . Hob had been out to the Kemper ranch just this morning. Maybe Matt wasn't aware of the poison that Hob spread about him behind his back. But Matt wouldn't tell him her secrets, anyway. He had promised, and all her instincts told her that Matt's word could be trusted. He wouldn't give her away.

Unless, of course, Hob Skinner was sly enough to run a successful bluff. With that wretched business card to back it up, he might make it work. He could show the card to Matt, claim that Jillian had told him the whole story, and ask what Matt was intending to do about the proposition? She didn't think Matt would be fooled, but he might inadvertently let something slip.

Jillian looked around and realized that she had unconsciously taken the turning that led in the direction of the Kemper ranch. Once she got there, she could tell Matt, warn him—beg him—to please, please not say one word to Hob Skinner about her or her business. Her foot pressed down hard on the accelerator.

Slow down, Jilly, she told herself. Let's not run around like a panicked chicken. Let's be sensible and think this thing out. For one thing, that miserable Hob Skinner could be following behind her this very minute. He'd be more than interested to find out where she was going in such a tearing hurry. She checked the rearview mirror. Nobody was in sight. She eased up further on the gas, dropping well below the speed limit. Hob Skinner would know the back roads and the shortcuts. What if she drove into Matt's place and Hob was there ahead of her? All of his suspicions would be confirmed.

She pulled onto the shoulder of the road and stopped. This headlong rush wasn't like her. She could handle her own problems, and without all this fuss. Why was she letting Hob Skinner frighten her like this? She took a deep breath. Whoa, Jilly, she told herself in the local vernacular. Steady down. Back up. Yes, definitely back up. In her motel room at the Wilderness Inn, there was a perfectly good telephone. She could speak to Matt Kemper quickly and privately—no matter where Hob Skinner happened to be lurking. One quick call to Matt would put him on the alert, and the breach in her defenses would be neatly repaired.

It was an excellent, nonpanicky plan of action, and Jillian felt pleased with herself for thinking of it. At least, she felt pleased until she dialed the number for the Kemper ranch as listed in the motel room directory, and the telephone rang unanswered on the other end.

She crossed her fingers and dialed again. With the same result. Could they all be working outside, every one of them? She had only seen Matt and the cook, but she assumed there were others. Surely the cook had to come back into the house to tend to his work. Hob Skinner could be out there this minute, smooth talking Matt out by the corrals.

Jillian paced the floor while she reconsidered her options. She could still dash out to the ranch. But if she found the house and surroundings deserted, she wouldn't have the faintest idea of where to look for Matt. He could be up in the hills. Anyplace. Maybe Hob Skinner wouldn't know where to look, either, and when everyone came back, they'd have to come in the house sometime. She would pin her hopes on Willy the cook being back soon, and stick to the telephone.

She forced herself to wait for three minutes before dialing again. Five minutes, the next time. She couldn't curb her impatience to stretch out the intervals longer than that during the long afternoon of waiting. Waiting and wondering if she had chosen the wrong course of action, after all. "Come on, Willy," she exhorted each time she dialed. "Be there!"

Light was fading from the evening sky before the receiver was picked up on the other end.

Matt lifted the phone and said, "Kemper ranch."

"Where in the world have you *been*?" she asked. Then, belatedly, as though realizing how her words had sounded, she went on, "I'm sorry, I just meant—I've been calling for quite a while...."

"We found a broken pipe at the other house," he said. "All of us have been down there trying to get it fixed. Is something wrong?"

"Did you—have you spoken to Hob Skinner? Has he been out to see you?" Her words tumbled out quickly, anxiously.

"Hob Skinner?" Matt gripped the receiver a little tighter. "No, he hasn't been here. What's he up to?"

"You haven't talked to him?"

"Not me. He did call up and get hold of Willy early this afternoon, just before we all left."

"What—what did he want?"

Now Matt understood her anxiety. "He was looking for some information about a Ms. Jillian Curtis. Wanted to know if that was the name of—let me remember, how did he describe you to Willy?—oh, yes, 'a little bitty gal with hair like a eggbeater full of whip cream.' A pretty good description, don't you think?"

"And did Willy tell him?" she asked quickly.

"You don't have to worry about Willy," Matt reassured her. "He's got no use for Hob. As he would say, he wouldn't tell Hob how many beans makes five."

"But what exactly *did* he tell him?" Jillian's voice sounded a little less strained, but not much.

"Something like . . . he didn't know what Hob was talking about, and not to bother him while he was cooking. Was that okay?"

"Oh, yes!" He heard her sigh of relief. "Perfect."

"What happened?" Matt asked, concerned. "How did you get mixed up with Hob Skinner?"

After a moment's hesitation, she said, "I was looking for a guide up into the mountains, and somebody gave me his name."

Matt frowned. "Somebody must be crazy, then. Hob's the last person I'd think of for a job like that."

"I realize that now." Her voice was rueful. "He was sort of thrown in as a last resort. But at least he didn't seem to have a wife and a big family to tell everybody where we were heading."

Matt guessed that made sense. Some, anyway. She couldn't have known what Hob was like, not until she actually ran into him. But what could Hob Skinner have done to Jillian to have her trying to get Matt on the phone all afternoon? "What's Hob up to?" he asked.

"Apparently he was driving out of your place this morning, and he saw me just as I turned onto your road from the highway. He tried to cross-examine me about what kind of business I had with you."

"And what did you tell him?"

"About as much as Willy did, I think. I tried to give him the idea that I was a tourist from the city looking for some horseback riding. But I don't think he believed that, not for a minute."

"You must have fooled him some," Matt said comfortingly. "If you left him not even knowing your name."

"Not really," she said in a small voice. "He got hold of one of my business cards."

Matt didn't like the sound of that. He couldn't see Jillian offering Hob Skinner a business card, not when their encounter had begun the way she had described. "How did he manage that?" he asked quietly.

She sighed again, then told him what had happened. "I didn't actually see him reach out his foot and knock my bag over, but that's what he must have done. He was none the wiser when he saw those pictures—they were just a few of the bad ones. For a minute he must have wondered if I was just the dizzy tourist I seemed to be—one who couldn't even hold a camera steady. Then he read my business card. And now I feel like I've got a bloodhound baying on my trail."

"Hob can do that to a person," Matt agreed. "But don't you worry. He didn't get any satisfaction out of Willy. And if he tries calling here again, I'll spin him some kind of story. Maybe I could convince him that nowadays Jillian is a man's name—out in the wide world that he knows nothing about. And so the card probably belongs to one of your boyfriends. And you're very attached to it for sentimental reasons."

She gave a wistful little chuckle. "Will he believe that?"

"You never can tell. It might be worth a try. I'd have to sound him out first, see if he ever heard the name before." Matt was pleased to hear that some of the strain had gone out of her voice. "Or I could just let Willy answer the phone."

"Either way, I'm sure the two of you can handle Hob Skinner. I'm just hoping he doesn't start following me around while I'm finding myself a proper trail guide."

"Listen, Jillian," Matt said seriously. "This trail guide idea isn't going to work. No matter who you hire."

"Why not?" There was a challenge in her voice.

"That's still Charley Alcott's property up there. Any reputable guide who sees those No Trespassing signs—and then the trees across the road—is going to know that Charley means business. He'll turn around and get out of there."

"But I plan to tell him to ignore the signs, that I absolutely have to see Mr. Alcott right away," Jillian countered.

"Are you planning on giving him a good reason?" Matt asked curiously.

"I'll tell him, for personal reasons," she said firmly.

"I'm sorry, Jillian, that's not going to be good enough. There must be some other way you can handle this. Couldn't you just call Charley on the telephone, or something?"

There was a silence on the other end of the line. "I didn't know he had a telephone up there," she said at last.

"He's even in the phone book. Just look up Alcott Lumber," Matt told her.

"We-e-ell," she said consideringly.

For a moment he thought she was going to listen to reason. Then she spoke and dashed his hopes.

"If I call up and ask him for permission to come and see him, and he turns me down, then I'm worse off than I was before. It's too easy to say no on the telephone."

"He might surprise you and agree," Matt pointed out, knowing he was fighting a losing battle.

"He won't, not if my experience with you is anything to go on," she retorted. "You just flatly didn't believe me at all, in the beginning. Isn't that right?"

"Well, maybe not entirely," he conceded. "But—"

"No, you didn't. It was a hard enough job convincing you in person," she said. "I wouldn't even try it over the telephone." There was a pause, as though she were thinking over his words. When she spoke again, her voice was brisk and businesslike. "I think you may be right—a guide would probably turn back when he sees what the situation is. In that case, I'll have to arrange to go alone."

"That's impossible," Matt said, alarmed.

"I don't see what's impossible about it," Jillian retorted. "There's a road to follow—I won't get lost. I just have to get around those trees in the way."

Matt felt his temper rising. "No one is going to be fool enough to let you have a horse to go off by yourself."

"You're the one who's always talking about horses." She sounded more sure of herself by the minute. "There are other ways of getting around, you know. I bet that a trail bike could simply circle around those trees and go right on up the road."

"Now, listen!" Matt heard himself shouting, and he forced himself to speak more calmly. "There is bound to be a second roadblock, much more serious than what we ran into. You won't get past the second one."

"You don't know that for certain."

"No, but I know how Charley's mind works. I'm telling you the truth."

"Even if you're right," Jillian said, "I still have to try. And if that doesn't work, I'll come back down and try something else."

"You're being pigheaded, and you know it!" Matt's voice was rising again.

"It's my job," Jillian said simply. "If someone tells *you* to leave a horse or cow alone because it's too tricky, I bet you just go ahead and figure out a way to handle it. That's all I'm doing."

"*Tricky* is not the word for this situation. You can get lost in those mountains. And that could be out-and-out *fatal*! I am not letting you go up there alone!"

There was a pause before she answered, and when she did her voice was polite and cool. "How do you propose to stop me?" she asked.

"I don't. It's plain that nothing could stop you. I'm going with you."

"Oh." The single syllable was loaded with surprise. Then, cautiously, "Well, I don't know. Not that it isn't a viable solution, but—"

"Don't talk to me about viable solutions!" he ordered. "Just keep quiet and listen. Give me the phone number where you are." He wrote it down as she complied. "All right. Now just stay put, and I'll see what I can do about getting a trail outfit together. Will you do that?"

"What time tomorrow do you want me to be ready to leave?" she asked.

"I'll have things to see to most of the day," he said. "We'll have to start out before sunrise to have any chance of doing the round-trip before nightfall. It'll be the day after tomorrow, at the earliest. I'll give you a call when I get the arrangements made."

"When will you call? What time?"

"When I get things taken care of." His voice was curt. Then he relented a little. "I'll be in touch with you sometime in the afternoon, probably late. Providing you don't go running off on your own before then."

"I won't," she said quietly. "I'll wait."

Matt hung up before he could say anything more that he would be sorry for. He stared down at the telephone, wondering if he had just been cleverly manipulated into insisting on doing something he never would have even considered if he was in his right mind. That talk about trail bikes and going alone—how much was true? Did she mean any of it? Or had he fallen for a clever con job?

Jillian replaced the receiver and gave a little pirouette of pleasure before she sat down on the edge of the motel bed. The rush of exhilaration she was feeling surprised her. It was wonderful to have solved the problem of how to get up to the logging camp. Of course it was. But even that would hardly account for the strange sensation under her breastbone.

She tried to analyze herself soberly. Was it apprehension? She was no great horsewoman, but she could certainly manage well enough for a trip like this. Or did she feel this way because she was going with Matt Kemper? That could have something to do with it, she conceded. Thinking of him brought back the sound of his voice, his final words. Judging by that, Matt certainly wasn't taking any pleasure in the prospect.

It *was* an imposition, she reflected, taking him away from his regular chores. Maybe even more of an imposition than she realized, if what Hob Skinner had said was true—if Matt was trying to make hard work take the place of money. But she was going to pay him, of course. Or DiCicco Productions would. Pay him for his time, and the rental of the horse. And anything else she could think of to pad the bill, Jillian decided, discarding a brief feeling of disloyalty to

Andrea. Matt would earn it. And the movie company would ultimately pay. She looked thoughtfully toward the telephone. Maybe he didn't understand that. Maybe she should call him back and tell him so. No, better not. She could do that tomorrow.

That harshness in his voice was hard to equate with the simple prospect of a lost day's work. Maybe Matt had a private reason for not wanting to approach Charley Alcott. Or was it that he had doubts of Jillian's sincerity when she proposed to tackle the mountain road by herself?

Her heart sank. From his viewpoint it could have appeared to be just a maneuver—and a pretty transparent one—to force him to give in and take her.

How exasperating! She had thought at the time that her trail bike idea was eminently sensible. And she still thought so. When each of her brothers had gone through the inevitable motorcycle phase, Jillian had never been content to ride pillion on the back. If the boys could learn to drive the hulking machines, so could she. And she did. If a trail bike could get up that mountain, Jillian was capable of riding it. And she'd probably manage the bike better than she would the darn horse that Matt would provide, she grumbled to herself.

She recognized what was going on. Matt Kemper was simply acting like most of the other men she had encountered in her life, assuming she was helpless. Well, maybe someday he would be able to look at her and see a capable flesh-and-blood woman, not some spun-glass fantasy that he had to carry around on a cushion.

She took herself out of that mood. There was nothing she could do to change his mind now. Right this minute she'd be better occupied in planning what she was going to do with her time until she heard from Matt tomorrow afternoon.

She lay back on the bed to think over her alternatives. She could drive around and get better acquainted with the town and whatever facilities it had to offer to a movie company,

such as restaurants and stores. But if Hob Skinner's curiosity hadn't been satisfied—and, of course, it hadn't—he
could be hanging around, waiting to waylay her in the middle of the main street. And around town it would be difficult to escape his notice. Driving the Porsche was like
waving a red flag and calling "Yoo-hoo, here I am!"

In the end, she decided to use the next morning to drive
the sixty-five miles back to La Grande and check out the
airport and car rental facilities in the area. The movie company was going to have reservations about that long drive.
They preferred to do their filming no more than thirty minutes from an airport that could handle four-engine planes.
Jillian could foresee that that was going to be an important
consideration when decision time finally arrived. Having
that one big drawback just made it vitally important that the
rest of the package should be perfect. Charley Alcott's locomotive could be the thing to tip the scales in their favor.

Late the next afternoon, Matt sat down with mixed emotions to dial Jillian's number. He told himself that he had
every right to be angry, letting himself be conned into
something like this by a pair of beguiling blue eyes and a
story any six-year-old could see through. It was just that a
baffling streak of anticipation seemed to have gotten mixed
up with all his righteous indignation.

Jillian's prompt and somewhat breathless response to the
telephone's first ring only added to that confusion. He made
his voice harsh as he said, "Everything's arranged. We leave
tomorrow morning."

"Wonderful!" she exclaimed. "I really appreciate this.
And I realize that we're taking advantage of you in keeping
you away from your work. But don't worry, we'll make it
worth your while."

That was a statement that could be interpreted in more
ways than one, Matt thought. "We'll have to start early,"
he told her. "Before daylight. Five o'clock."

"I'll be there," she said stoutly.

Matt doubted it. She looked more like a ten o'clock riser to him. "You could spend the night here," he suggested tentatively, curious to hear her reaction.

"Good idea." She sounded delighted. "That will save me a drive in the morning."

Not an instant's hesitation, he thought. She hadn't even paused to wonder if she'd have to fend off unwelcome advances if she accepted his invitation. That cheerful self-assurance made him want to shake her. Didn't she know that wicked dragons are always on the prowl after fairy-tale princesses? If she was looking on him as some kind of faithful old sheepdog who could be counted on never to present any problems, then maybe she had another think coming. Maybe he was feeling pretty dragonish himself.

"Are you still there?" she asked.

"Come for dinner," he said abruptly.

"I don't want to be too much of a bother...."

"No bother. Willy's got it all in the oven, anyway," he said ungraciously. He was sorely tempted not to mention that Willy and the hands had already gone back to the other house. It would be interesting to wait and tell her after she arrived. That way he could watch her eyes as she bumped up against reality for once, when she suddenly realized she'd be spending the night alone with him.

"Willy only came back for a while, to tend to the cooking," he said coldly. "Everyone's staying at the other house, digging up that broken pipe."

"I suppose that's where *you* would be, if it wasn't for my taking up your time." He heard sympathy in her voice; she seemed to have missed his point completely.

"How long do you think this trip will take us?" she said.

"I wouldn't even guess," he said, exasperation making the words harsh again. "Not without seeing what Charley's done to the road. It could be simple, just an easy five- or six-hour ride—"

He thought he heard a smothered protest from her end of the line. Six hours on a horse might not be her idea of easy. He went on, "Or we could have to backtrack and circle around for a couple of days."

"Oh my," she said, and paused. "That would mean camping out?"

"That's right. I'm taking a packhorse and the camp outfit, just in case."

"That doesn't sound so bad."

Matt had a sudden conviction that they were sharing the same vision—a flickering camp fire, sizzling steaks...

"I'll bring the marshmallows," Jillian volunteered.

"You'd do better to bring your long underwear," he said repressively. "It can get cold up there at night. Do you have any warm clothes with you?"

"I'll be fine. I brought my ski parka. It's good to ten below zero. I think I'll pack everything up and drive out now. I only hope that I can sneak away without Hob Skinner finding out. I've been keeping a low profile all day, so no one would notice me."

Matt had to smile at that. As though she could ever not be noticed. Her kind of small golden perfection carried its own illumination, its own spotlight. That fragile porcelain beauty would turn heads anywhere. And add to that her flashy expensive car...

"Come out whenever you're ready," Matt said. "We'll put the Porsche under cover to keep it out of sight. But I don't think Hob will be dropping around for another visit."

As Jillian drove up the road to the ranch house, she saw Matt walk out of the stable and look up to the sound of the car's engine. The sun was half-hidden behind the rim of the western mountains, and Matt's tall figure cast a long shadow that blended with the other shadows welling up from the valley floor. For some reason the sight of him rekindled that spark of exhilaration she had felt after their long telephone conversation.

He didn't raise his hand in greeting, just stood and watched her approach. She braked in front of him, and he motioned her to drive on toward a small shed with double doors, which were pushed wide open. Unsmiling, his eyes enigmatic, he waited as she unlocked the trunk, then lifted out her small overnight bag.

"Where's the rest?"

"The rest of what?" she asked.

"Your suitcases."

"This is all there is." Jillian was dressed much the same as she had been the day before: boots, jeans, shirt and scarf, with the addition of a light windbreaker because the evening was cool. She carried her oversize bag slung over one shoulder, and a bright red parka was draped over her arm. "I travel light." She wondered if he had expected her to turn up with a set of matched luggage and a hatbox. She searched his set face for some sign of welcome.

"I did tell you that everyone's away—working on that broken pipe," he said, making it half a question.

I'm just a nuisance to him, she thought ruefully. A waste of valuable time. Naturally he's not thrilled to be dragged away from the work he needs to get done. Especially if he really is having a hard time financially, like Hob Skinner said. She had a sudden wild impulse to pull Matt's tanned cheek down against her own and assure him that everything was going to be all right. That she, Jillian, would *make* it all right. That she would personally squeeze every last nickel out of the movie company when they came to negotiate for the use of the Kemper ranch.

But of course she couldn't do that. Instead, she said, "I understand. And we *will* make it up to you. It's going to be worth your while."

He scowled and looked away, leaving her to study his lean profile and will him to be glad of her presence.

She was sure that he, too, felt the attraction that flowed between them like an electric current. The air fairly sparked with it. Her own body felt strange to her, alive in ways it had never been before. She was overwhelmingly aware of his body so close to hers, of its strength and masculinity. But those clenched hands, that set jawline, added up to a very discouraging barrier. Still, she had never been the type to keep quiet and fold her hands when she met a problem.

"I love your mountains." She looked up at him intently, making it plain that he was expected to reply to this conversational gambit.

"You have higher mountains than this back home," Matt said shortly.

"That's true, but Mount Hood is fifty miles from town, and we're down so low, and it's up so high . . ." She tried to put her feelings into words. "It's different here. In a high valley like this, the mountains seem to sort of wrap themselves around you. It feels like they're looking over your shoulder. It's—it's more neighborly."

He threw her a quick glance. "You think the Wallowas are neighborly?"

"Most things are, if you meet them halfway." There, she couldn't say it any plainer than that. She had never, ever experienced this kind of problem before. Never known anyone so tall and gorgeous who could make her skin tingle and her heart go thump—and who just persisted in seeming angry and depressed by her presence.

Matt looked at her longer this time. Much longer. His eyes changed. A light had kindled behind them. A rather bold disturbing light that left her even more uncomfortable than before.

Chapter Five

Matt ushered Jillian into a kitchen filled with savory odors. He set the overnight bag down just inside the door. "I have to finish seeing to the horses," he said, and left her quickly, almost as though he were making an escape.

Jillian looked after him with perplexity. He could have at least stayed to indicate which room was to be hers. She picked up the light suitcase and carried it into the hallway with an undaunted air. She would surely recognize a guest bedroom when she saw one.

The doors on each side of the long central hall were all ajar, so she didn't have to open each one and feel as though she were prying.

Her room would hardly be the small cluttered one that opened off the kitchen. That would be Willy's. And not the big brown masculine one with a saddle in one corner. Ah, here was an unused-looking room with a patchwork quilt on the bed and windows that faced the neighboring mountains, promising a glorious view of the coming sunset.

Jillian took possession. She opened her suitcase and laid out her robe and nightgown on the bed. Then she combed her hair in front of the round mirror on the dresser, all the while listening intently for the sound of Matt's return.

When she was done, there was still no sign of Matt, and she wandered down the long hallway into the living room, where she had shared doughnuts and coffee with him on that first golden day. Was that only yesterday? It seemed like a century had passed since she'd walked through the heavy oak door and discovered everything she had been searching for. That time she had gazed around her with dazzled eyes. Perhaps now she could make a more balanced appraisal.

The room was reasonably clean and tidy, considering that only men lived in it. But it was obvious that quite a few years had gone by since it had experienced a woman's touch. Or had any money spent on it. Her fingers itched for a paint-brush, window cleaner, draperies to hang. What a mellow welcoming haven she could make of a room like this.

She blinked as though awakening from sleep, surprised at where her musing had taken her. What was she doing, standing here mentally redecorating a stranger's house? Not that Matt seemed like a stranger, really. In some ways...

She reined in her wandering thoughts again. Enough of that. It was time to do something practical. Such as get back to the kitchen. It was beginning to look as though she was elected to get dinner on the table.

The sun had nearly disappeared behind the mountains. Jillian found the light switch and surveyed the largest kitchen she had ever been in. There was a big old wood stove, just as she had expected, and right beside it a white porcelain one that apparently used more modern fuel. It was from the latter that the savory smells emanated.

She lifted pot lids, opened the oven door and peered in-side. A roast as big as the side of a cow cooked gently, po-tatoes and carrots browning around it. In one pot was enough baked beans to feed a threshing crew. There was fresh-baked bread on the long drain board, along with two kinds of pie: apple and berry.

Jillian shook her head ruefully. In any cooking contest with Willy, it looked like she'd be down with the also-rans. Of course, he might not be an expert at making chocolate mousse. Or quiche.

When Matt opened the door from the back porch, she turned around with a start—though all she had been doing was investigating the contents of the refrigerator.

Matt sniffed the rich aromas of the cooking food. "Willy's not here, so we can't offer you any hot biscuits tonight," he said rather cheerlessly.

For just a moment, a vision flashed before Jillian's eyes of herself standing in the kitchen in a little ruffled apron, with a blue mixing bowl and a panful of perfect mouthwatering brown biscuits. She, Jillian Curtis, actually tossed off tender fluffy biscuits all the time. Unfortunately, she made them with packaged biscuit mix. The vision vanished. Someone who baked his own bread wasn't likely to buy biscuit mix in a box.

"That's too bad," she said with a guileless smile. "But I see he's left us quite enough without them."

Matt opened the oven door, surveyed the contents of the open roasting pan and held out a commanding hand in her direction. Jillian correctly interpreted the wordless gesture, and scooped up a pair of pot holders and placed them in his grasp.

"I'll take this out for you," he said, suiting the action to the words. "The platters are in the cupboard by the door."

Jillian smiled sweetly and forbore to mention that any good housewife would have had the pot holders and platters at hand before tackling a chunk of meat that size.

"I'll lift this out now," he said, "and come back and make the gravy after I've washed up."

Jillian selected a platter and silently counted to ten as she brought it to the stove. Did the man have to take it for granted that she was completely useless? "I think I can manage to make gravy," she said with deceptive meekness.

He gave her a swift glance, but if he detected a trace of sarcasm, he gave no sign. He carried the heavy roast over to the long table with its red-checked tablecloth, then turned and left the kitchen without another word.

Jillian gazed after him, perplexed. Any other man she knew would have considered that little interlude of domestic intimacy the ideal lead-in to a kiss. At the very least. And most men would have inspired nothing but evasive action from her.

It wasn't that he was indifferent to her as a woman, either. Every nerve in her body knew that he was as painfully aware of her as she was of him.

She looked around the brightly lighted kitchen. The strictly utilitarian table would easily handle a dozen hearty eaters, maybe eighteen or twenty at a pinch. Well, she and Matt would just camp out at one end of the long expanse of checkered calico. For this meal, at least. She gave up on a dreamy vision of firelight and candles that had somehow persisted at the back of her mind. No warm encircling shadows for them tonight, no intimate oasis for two....

It's practical little housewife time, Jilly, she told herself silently, so get busy. It's potatoes-and-gravy time right here under the bright lights and in the middle of the pots and pans.

When Matt came out of his room, he paused in the shadows of the hallway, watching her bright head bent over the battered roasting pan as she concentrated on stirring lumps out of the gravy. Her presence transformed the humdrum kitchen. Just by being there, she brought spring flowers and sunrise and soft music into the practical well-worn surroundings. She looked so right, standing there in her jeans and boots with an air of being engrossed in her task. And yet, all the things he knew about her told him that he couldn't be more wrong. The red car, the glamorous lifestyle, her whole lovely expensive facade told him that this was all a pose. She really belonged in front of the camera, with acting talent like that. Where she would be even more unobtainable than she was now. Well, if it *was* an act, he wanted to know how far she would carry it, to what lengths she was prepared to go.

He strode onto the well-worn linoleum of the kitchen, and she stiffened slightly at the sound of his footsteps. She stirred the gravy more vigorously and said without turning around, "Have I been looking in the wrong place for trouble?"

He stopped dead. "What are you talking about?"

"It just occurred to me that with all this hurly-burly over getting the railroad, you never actually said you'd let us use the ranch. . . ." Her voice trailed off questioningly.

"I don't think it makes any difference." There was a rough edge to his words. "When Charley turns you down, that will scuttle the whole project."

She turned to face him, pink with heat and anger. "I may not have handled this very professionally so far, but I don't intend to make any more mistakes. The company's negotiators know their business. When they get through, Charley will sign on the dotted line."

His hands reached out for her, grasping her shoulders. "What do you mean, you don't intend to make any *more* mistakes?"

"I should never have said anything to you about the movie being made here. Never. If Andrea knew how I opened my mouth and let it all out, she'd say it was the worst thing I could have done. I've ruined the chance for secrecy, driven up the prices—"

Now his arms slid around her comfortingly, encircled her and drew her close to his tall frame, her cheek against his chest. Her rigid body became pliant and molded itself to his.

"Then your Andrea would be crazy. Maybe she can get away with these things in the city, but not out here. When you're twenty miles from nowhere, you can't drive up to a man's front steps and start snapping pictures without answering some pointed questions about what you're doing. You know that your secret is safe with me. I'm not going to tell them you let the cat out of the bag. And if they're going to blame you if I turn down their lowest offer, well—''

"No, no, I don't mean that at all! Of *course* you have to make them pay you—pay you well—for all your trouble." She started to push herself away, but he held her fast. After a moment she relaxed and surrendered to the warmth of his embrace.

"What is the problem, then?" His voice was gently mocking, inviting her to laugh at her fears.

"*Will* you let us use the ranch?"

He paused for a moment, then chose his words carefully. "If Charley agrees to let you use the railroad, I'll let you rent the ranch."

"Never mind what Charley does. Leave him out of it. Will you sign the contract?"

"If your movie company is still interested, I'll sign."

She sighed. "Can't you just say that you will, without adding a lot of 'ifs'?"

"The world is full of 'ifs,'" he said, and bent to kiss her. A tiny voice somewhere whispered to him that he had just been neatly manipulated into an agreement he hadn't intended to commit himself to, but he stilled its message with the sweetness of her lips.

Jillian closed her eyes and let herself be borne away on a delicious flood of sensation, one so new, so unexpectedly strong, that all the emotions she had previously felt for Matt were now shriveled in its fire. Attraction, affection, protectiveness—those were all tame emotions. Now they had been touched by flame, transmuted into something wild and fierce that claimed her in a way she had never experienced before.

Time passed or stood still or turned back on itself, as they stood unheeding, bodies molded together. They were outside of time, the world, the universe.

At last they drew apart slightly, gazing at each other through passion-dazed eyes. He effortlessly swung her up into his arms. She was between heaven and earth, weightless, powerless, totally unable to protest. Unable, and unwilling. She had no will, only desire, a slumbering fire unleashed at last.

A strong smell of something burning penetrated their drugged senses.

"Oh my gosh, the gravy!" Jillian exclaimed.

"Damn the gravy!" Matt growled. But he reluctantly lowered her to her feet.

They turned back to the stove to survey the damage.

Saved by the gravy, Jillian thought privately as she seized a pot holder and pulled the roasting pan from the burner. Saved, whether she really wanted to be or not. The roaring in her blood slowly subsided, the strange wildness within her sheathed its claws. She kept her head down and shakily dabbed a spoon at the scorched mess on the inside of the pan.

"Leave it," he said, his voice still a little unsteady.

"Yes, it's beyond saving," she answered a bit too brightly. "Goodness knows, there's more than enough to eat without it. From the size of the roast, Willy must have expected a couple of football teams to drop in for dinner."

"That's for the sandwiches." Matt's voice was under control now. "Something to eat on the trail tomorrow."

Jillian glanced out the window at the waiting mountains. The sun had disappeared, and the peaks stood out as black silhouettes against a darkening sky. She felt a little chill.

She sat down quickly, putting the corner of the table between herself and Matt. She searched for an impersonal topic of conversation. "Are your men sleeping out under the cold stars tonight?"

He started to carve the roast into thick juicy slices. "Not them. They'll bunk down at the old Skinner house."

She raised her eyebrows. "The Skinner house?"

"Hob's old place. Mine, now. The south half of the Kemper ranch for the past eight years," he said with a sardonic twist of his lips and a bitterness in his voice that closed the subject.

Talk between them limped after that. It was as though they were both groping their way back from a precipice that had proved to be more dizzying than they had expected. The slight constraint lasted even after the dishes were washed. Jillian was grateful that they had to be up before dawn, since she could use that as an excellent excuse to go to bed very early.

She turned over restlessly in the guest room bed, punching at the pillow.

"At least we know the physical attraction is there," she told the unheeding room. "Talk about playing with fire. That kiss was like tossing a torch into an oil well. Where Matt's concerned, there's no need for candlelight."

Jillian shivered inside her red ski parka as she shut the kitchen door behind her and started toward the stables. At five o'clock in the morning, the sky was still pitch-black and the air was numbing cold. There was no moon evident, but a glorious canopy of stars lighted her path, stars that seemed to hang closer, thicker, brighter than in any city sky she had ever seen.

Golden light streamed onto the ground as Matt pushed open the stable door and led out a sleek chestnut horse with a white blaze on its face. Man and horse stopped beside a large aluminum trailer already hitched to the pickup truck.

Matt looked surprised to see her standing there. Jillian felt a small twinge of satisfaction, one that dispelled some of the chagrin she had felt at getting out of bed before five o'clock only to find that he had preceded her. Not only were his breakfast dishes drying in the sink, but great chunks of the roast were missing, and she knew that he had already packed the food for the trail.

She wanted to ask him why he hadn't wakened her, why he hadn't waited to eat breakfast with her. She had a half-coherent feeling that sitting bleary-eyed across from each other, sharing that first cup of coffee in the morning, would prove something about their situation—one way or another.

Instead she said, "What a beautiful horse."

He led the handsome animal up to her. "Meet Mufrrin. I borrowed him just for you."

She held out her hand. Mufrrin bowed his head, then raised it again when he saw the hand was empty.

Matt laughed. He dug in a pocket of the padded vest he wore and gave her a sugar cube. "He's used to pretty girls admiring him and bringing him treats."

Jillian offered the sugar on the flat of her hand and felt the horse's warm breath on her skin as his lips daintily touched her palm. "Mufrrin," she crooned to the alert ears.

"He's an Arabian," Matt said. "He's got an Arab name a yard long. Mufrrin for short. Best trained riding horse in the valley. Best ladies' horse, too. He'll take care of you."

"Mufrrin," Jillian said again as the horse stood poised and still, outlined in light. "What does his name mean?"

"I don't know. Maybe nothing. I'll have to ask Peggy when I take him back."

"Peggy?" Jillian felt her eyebrows draw together in a frown, then hastened to remove the telltale expression.

"He's Peggy Upshaw's prize horse. The trailer belongs to her, too. Mine won't take three horses."

"Three?" Jillian asked vaguely, her attention taken up with speculation about this Peggy Upshaw person, with her fancy horse and trailer.

"We have to have a pack animal, since we don't know what we'll run into along the trail up there. As soon as you get your things together, we'll head out."

"I don't plan on taking much," she said. "I usually just stuff everything into that big bag of mine."

"Well, Mufrrin's good-natured, but I don't know as he'd take to a rider carrying a purse. Here, take his saddlebags. Put whatever you want to take in them. If anything's left over, it can go in the pack."

He hung the leather bags over her arm. She trudged back to the house with them, a little dubious. Once she started packing, she was surprised at how much they would hold. Anyway, she thought, she wouldn't need much, not for a trip that would last overnight at the very longest. A change of underthings. Extra cotton boot socks. Another blue cotton work shirt. *Not* the little knit jersey dress that rolled up into a ball and went everywhere in the corner of her bag. Not the dress slacks or the white wool blazer or the velvet blouse. Not much use for them up on the mountainside.

Too bad she hadn't brought pajamas, if a sleeping bag under the stars was a possibility. Her T-shirt would have to do to sleep in—the nightgown and robe would be just too tenderfoot for words. Makeup and hairbrush. And the camera, of course. The whole purpose of the expedition was to get pictures of Charley Alcott's railroad. There was still plenty of room for her light windbreaker, her big black business book, a package of marshmallows and other odds and ends. In a matter of minutes she had made her selections and finished her packing. She hung the smooth leather bags over her left shoulder and, with a stab of trepidation she refused to acknowledge, went out to face the mountains. And Mufrrin. And Matt.

The cold outside air was like a bracing slap-in-the-face tonic. In contrast, once they were on their way, the warmth of the truck cab was almost cosy. Jillian found herself relaxing against the seat cushions. They drove along in a trancelike silence, as though the world of the night was not yet ready to release them to the exuberance of the morning. Gradually the sky began to shade from utter blackness into imperceptibly lightening hues of gray. The brilliant stars paled. Individual objects began to emerge from the formless darkness and assemble themselves into recognizable features of the landscape. Then they left the open valley and plunged into the shadows of the trees, and blackness closed in again, but only for a brief moment. The rising sun dissolved the last of the night as it lighted up the eastern sky and painted the world in broad strokes of color.

Matt drove slowly, easing the truck over the worst of the narrow road, finally braking to a stop in the clearing where the two felled trees blocked the way. Jillian stepped out into the clean bright morning, and all at once she was wide awake.

The forest hush, the freshness of the air, the resilience of pine needles underfoot, all combined to give her a feeling of lightness and happiness, a rush of heady joy. Some of that, she realized, could surely be attributed to the presence of Matt, so tall and competent-looking as he went about the task of unloading the animals from the trailer. Matt's horse was a heavy-boned gray, bigger than Mufrrin and, to Jillian's eyes, not nearly so elegant. The gray horse snorted and danced at the end of his halter, in spite of Matt's steadying hands.

"Settle down, Harper!" Matt told him sharply. The big horse snorted again, then stood quivering as Matt saddled him, his breath making little plumes of white in the cold air.

"He looks like he's breathing fire," Jillian remarked.

Matt flashed her a brief grin, then shook his head. His expression combined pride in his spirited animal with a touch of sheepishness. For a moment she couldn't listen to Matt's words, not with her heart turning over at the look of him. A girl could die for a smile like that.

"Harper's always a handful on a frosty morning," he was saying. "Got to get the kinks out and get the blood flowing. But I'm afraid he's got more than that on his mind today. He and Mufrrin don't seem to like each other very much."

She was surprised. "I didn't know horses had likes and dislikes."

He grinned again. Her heart turned over again. He said, "They're human, too."

She smiled back at him. "What did they do, have a political argument in the trailer on the way up?"

"That's not so farfetched as you think. They're both used to being boss horse in their own territory."

"And whose territory are we in now?"

His grin faded abruptly. "I guess this is Charley Alcott's territory." He slapped the gray horse's flank. "Move over, Harp."

Jillian started to say that in that case it looked like the Iron Horse was boss around here, but she thought better of it and kept silent. It was a slender joke, but in other circumstances Matt might have gotten a smile out of it. They did seem to laugh at the same things. But, for the moment at least, he was in no mood for levity. Perhaps she could tell it to him later, when the unpleasant part of the trip was over and done with, and they were coming out the other side. Railroad, iron horse, boss horse. Not all that funny, maybe, she thought dispiritedly. Or maybe she should try it on Mr. Alcott. She sighed, realizing that she had been thinking about Matt and this ride with him to the exclusion of everything else. She had hardly even considered what might be waiting for them at the end of the trail. She crossed her fingers and made a silent prayer to the universe: Please let Charley Alcott be far away when we get there.

Mufrrin was as steady as a rock when she mounted, and Jillian was able to swing up into the saddle without disgracing herself. Matt shortened the stirrups to fit her. Then he mounted Harper, picked up the packhorse's rope and turned toward the fallen trees.

They followed the road as it wound upward. It was almost too easy. They trotted along at a comfortable pace, side by side, meeting no new obstructions. Matt was taciturn at first, watching Jillian's horsemanship critically, saying little except "Lean forward on the uphill" or "Brace yourself in the stirrups going down." Jillian wished that they were headed anywhere but their actual destination. The sky above their heads was a clear cloudless blue. It could have been so perfect; the two of them alone together in a place like this, on a day like this.

As the sun's rays strengthened, dispelling the frosty nip of night, Matt's attitude softened, too. His watchful eyes seemed more concerned than critical. He called for a coffee stop much earlier than she would have done.

She dismounted into the security of his steadying hands at her waist. For a moment neither of them moved as the reality of their surroundings was submerged in the reality of their closeness. Then his hands dropped away. He turned back to rummage in his saddlebags for a Thermos of coffee and a sack of doughnuts.

With no clop of horses' hooves or creak of saddle leather to break the stillness, the sound of rushing water came plainly to their ears. Jillian cocked her head to listen better. He saw the gesture and interpreted it correctly.

"The snows are melting. Streams are full this time of year."

They sat on a fallen log to eat. The packhorse came up and stood nearby, his head hanging.

"Poor thing," said Jillian sympathetically.

"Poor thing my eye," Matt retorted. "Don't let him kid you. That pack doesn't even weigh as much as you do. A couple of down sleeping bags, some pots and food and tarps. He's just doggone lucky that he doesn't have to carry *me*."

She glanced at his rangy well-knit frame, then quickly looked away.

"Old Swallow's a natural con artist," he went on. "The only time he ever travels at speed is when he's heading for home."

"Swallow?" she said. "As in, take a bite of doughnut and swallow it?"

He laughed. "Swallow, as in bird, the kind that come back to Capistrano every year. Anytime he gets loose, he goes hell-for-leather for the home pasture."

Jillian studied the woebegone-looking horse. "I suppose you could have called him Pigeon. As in homing."

"It's a thought. We could always change it. Shall we hunt up the steam and baptize him in icewater?"

"Then the poor thing *would* have something to complain about. And he'd have to get used to a new name."

"That wouldn't make any difference. He doesn't answer to it, anyway. Not like Mufrrin, eh, boy?"

Mufrrin pricked his ears forward and looked interested. Jillian sighed with contentment. "I confess I was a little nervous about this ride. You made it sound pretty grim. But so far it's been lovely."

A cloud passed over Matt's face. "We haven't gotten there yet. There's plenty of time for things to go wrong."

They moved on, and the road continued to unroll itself harmlessly in front of them. Twice it spanned shallow noisy streams on perfectly sound small bridges. For the most part, they were hemmed in closely by the dark ponderosa pines, but at irregular intervals they would ride out into sunny clearings. In one of these open spaces they ate their lunch—thick sandwiches of roast beef spread with mustard and crumbly slices of apple pie.

Jillian took the opportunity to trade her padded jacket for her light windbreaker. The air was increasingly warm, even though they were climbing steadily, and there was just enough breeze to maintain a brisk sparkle to the day.

A short distance up the road, they rounded a bend and came upon another barricade, this time an impenetrable one. Here the going was steep and the road had been literally carved into the side of the mountain. Their future progress was effectively barred by another pair of felled trees that blocked their path and filled the road with a dark tangle of trunks and branches. This time there would be no going around them, for the cliff rose straight up on one side and plunged straight down on the other.

"Now what will we do?" Jillian was concerned, but not dismayed. She had every confidence in Matt's ability to deal with the situation. He would have been expecting this, or something like it.

He sized up the terrain with narrowed eyes, then headed Harper around the way they had come. "We'll have to backtrack a little, find a better spot to take to the trees and circle around."

After a short time of picking their way through the forest on their own, Jillian began to feel a new appreciation for the comparative comfort of the blacktopped road. How much easier it had been to duck the tree branches back there. Branches that were now plucking at her hair, raking along the horses' sides, catching at her clothes. The ground underfoot was softer here but tangled and uneven, so that she pitched forward and back and had to clutch at the saddle horn. She felt a little embarrassed, but she accepted that as the lesser evil. It would be infinitely worse to fall off.

It was also the end of riding side by side with Matt. They were reduced to going single file up the steep slope. Even Mufrrin seemed edgy and harder to handle, here at the end of the line. He continually crowded forward on Swallow's heels. The first time they came to a clearing, he forged ahead, passing Swallow, coming up on the left of Matt on the big gray. Mufrrin quickened his pace even further, but the heavier horse veered left and shouldered him back. Mufrrin tossed his head as he was forced to drop behind. In a few minutes he inched forward again, in spite of all that Jillian could do to stop him.

She pulled on the reins, but she didn't have the skill or the authority to make the Arabian do her bidding. For the first time she realized the size and strength of the animal beneath her.

"What's going on?" she cried as Mufrrin carried her up alongside of Matt once more.

Matt's voice boomed out suddenly. "Get back, Mufrrin!"

The brown horse checked its stride.

"What am I doing wrong?" she asked. "All of a sudden he won't do anything I want him to."

Matt turned in the saddle and saw her ineffectually sawing at the reins. "It's not your fault. Muffrin's been brought up to believe that he's supposed to be the lead horse. You, Mufrrin," he said in a voice of total authority, "get back there and mind your manners. I'm ashamed of you."

The horse understood his tone, if not the words. He stood like a stone until Swallow passed him, then fell in behind with a slow collected gait. Jillian loosened her death grip on the reins, but only slightly. She knew nothing of horse psychology, but some tension in Mufrrin's body communicated itself to her. She had the feeling that if he had been a big cat, he would have been twitching his tail ominously.

Chapter Six

Matt looked back over his shoulder, watching Jillian. The going was rougher than he'd expected it to be, but she was following along gamely. For a city girl, she was doing exceptionally well. For some reason, that made him feel proud, even though she wasn't his to take pride in. As soon as they found the smallest clearing in these pines, he would call another rest stop to give her a breathing space. He reined Harper in, changing direction slightly so that they were no longer making so much upward progress but were angling off to the right. Somewhere ahead their path should intersect with the railroad tracks. If they could find the tracks, they could ride parallel with them the rest of the way into the logging camp.

It was a full thirty minutes before they came to a break in the trees, a long narrow cut where the sun shone through in a thin straight line. Matt pulled Harper to a stop. Mufrrin surged ahead, ignoring low-hanging tree branches that impeded his progress and threatened to brush Jillian out of the saddle. Her efforts to hold the horse back were ineffec-

tual. She ducked her head and put up her arm to protect her
face from the slashing pine needles.

"Mufrrin, stop!" she cried.

Matt swore and snatched at the brown horse's reins. Mufrrin's head came around, and he quivered to a stop in
Matt's grasp, shoulder to shoulder with his rival.

Matt took a firmer rein on Harper and moved the gray
horse sideways to give himself room to dismount.

He reached up to help Jillian down. This time she leaned
against him a little more heavily than before—two feathers'
weight instead of one—and he realized fully just how long
and difficult the ride had been for a tenderfoot. But her blue
eyes were still sunny, and there was no trace of complaint in
her voice.

"Where are we now?" she asked, looking around at the
gap in the trees.

"We've come across the remains of an old logging road."
He pointed out the ruts in the ground, now mostly covered
with scrubby underbrush.

She stretched her body gingerly, glancing along the narrow slash that cut through the forest. "It's nice to be out in
the open, even for just a few minutes." She cast a quick look
at the shadowy gloom beneath the close-standing trees just
a few yards away. Though she said no more, he understood
what she was feeling.

"We can ride along this track. It's going in the same
direction we want to go. It might take us all the way into the
logging camp. It should at least cut across the railroad
somewhere." He poured her a cup of coffee and indicated
a moldering log at the edge of the trees. "You could sit
down there, if you like."

She took the coffee and gave him a rueful smile.
"Thanks, but I think I had better stand." Holding the cup,
she walked into the center of the road and turned her face
up to the sunshine, basking like a cat in its mild springtime
warmth.

Because her eyes were closed, he could stand there and look down on her openly. And he thought how small she was, and how gallant. Charley Alcott had better treat this girl decently. Or else.

She opened her eyes and saw him staring down at her with a troubled look on his face.

Her immediate impulse was to clutch his arm and reassure him that everything was perfectly fine. But she restrained herself for two reasons. First, because she supposed that his concern was for her physical condition, and she would be less than truthful if she insisted that she wasn't at all stiff and sore from the unaccustomed hours in the saddle. The second, more important, reason was that she remembered with photographic clarity what had happened both of the other times they had touched like that. The world had turned into a different place as their bodies kindled to each other. And each time, when the moment had passed, Matt had turned into a moody stranger.

The last thing she wanted to do was to spoil the sweetness, the specialness of this day. So she merely smiled and silently finished her coffee. From somewhere off to the right came the familiar murmur and chuckle of fast-moving water.

She cocked her head to listen. "Is that the same stream we heard before, or a different one?"

His expression lightened as he made an effort to match her mood. "That's something we may never know," he said. "There's more than one creek running down the mountainside this time of year. They mostly all look alike, fast and rocky and shallow." He collected her cup and began to pack up the Thermos, preparing to move on.

Jillian looked with some apprehension at Mufrrin. His ears were pricked forward, and she knew that she was going to have her hands more than full trying to hold him in line for the rest of the ride.

Matt followed the direction of her glance as he came over to help her mount. He handed her the reins and slapped Mufrrin's neck lightly. Mufrrin dipped his head and raised it again, as though answering a question in the affirmative.

Jillian said, "I hope that means he's ready to be agreeable and walk at the end of the line without making any more fuss."

"Maybe he won't have to bring up the rear," Matt answered. "There's just about room here for the two of us to ride side by side."

"Thank goodness. That should solve the problem." She was both relieved and pleased. It would be infinitely more fun to ride next to Matt, to talk together—and be silent together—through the rest of this golden afternoon.

Unfortunately, Mufrrin refused to cooperate. He seemed unwilling to forgive and forget his previous humiliation. For a while he would pace docilely in step with Harper, then, little by little, his neck would stretch out, his stride lengthening, until Jillian hauled back on the reins with all the authority she could muster. This persistent annoyance began to rub some of the gloss from the day, dispersing the dreamlike camaraderie she had felt between Matt and herself when they had started out this morning.

She glanced sideways at Matt, studying him covertly, trying to decide whether he was having a similar problem with Harper. No, definitely not, she concluded at last. He had too much strength of arm and shoulder, too secure an air of command, for him to have to put up with any such antics from his mount.

She shivered slightly. The little ribbon of sunlight that made its way through the break in the trees seemed to have lost some of its strength; the dark shadows cast by the pines now held a definite chill.

"You're cold," he said, surprising her. He must be as aware of her as she was of him. She wondered if he'd been watching her all the while she was watching him.

She said, "The sun's still shining, but it doesn't seem nearly as warm as it was before."

"We've been climbing pretty steadily. The air's cooler at this altitude. And it's going to get cooler yet once the sun gets behind that ridge over there."

"I didn't realize the day was so far along." A sudden thought struck her. "Will we get to the logging camp before dark?"

"There's no way of telling," Matt said. "We're headed in the right direction, but we've had to come at it in a roundabout way. The camp could be one mile up this road—or fifteen. But the day isn't as far gone as it looks from here. If we were on top of the ridge instead of down here below it, it would seem like there's still a fair chunk of daylight left. But it's not going to get any warmer. Maybe it's time for another layer of clothes."

She hugged the windbreaker closer around her. The thin material was cold against her arms. Matt was right: she did need something more to wear. But her muscles were beginning to tire, and she no longer felt quite secure in the saddle. To get out the other jacket meant she would have to shift her weight to get into the saddlebags, and lean and twist to exchange one for the other. And to dismount and mount again seemed to call for more effort than she cared to expend right now. "I'll be all right," she said quickly.

Matt reined Harper to a stop and halted Mufrrin with a commanding word. He swung to the ground as effortlessly as though he had spent the day in a rocking chair instead of in a saddle. "Did you bring a sweater?" he said.

"I guess I'd better have my ski jacket." She was beginning to realize that he hadn't been kidding when he suggested she bring her long underwear. She just hadn't taken him seriously. Neither had she quite believed that there was a chance they might be camping for the night along the trail. That skeptical attitude—plus her own penchant for traveling light—had resulted in Jillian finding herself rather uncharacteristically unprepared. She was afraid that she had let herself in for some chilly hours ahead. But she couldn't make herself worry too much about that. Not with Matt looking out for her the way he was doing right now—folding her discarded windbreaker into the half-empty saddlebag while she thrust her arms into the comfort of the padded sleeves of her bright red ski jacket. The chilliness disappeared almost immediately, and she let the jacket hang open. She'd wait to zip it up until the temperature dropped a few more degrees.

"That feels great." She smiled down at him. "Thank you. You'd make a wonderful wilderness guide."

His answering smile faded suddenly. It seemed to cost him an effort to keep his voice light when he replied. "Maybe I'll call on you for a testimonial when I take up guiding dudes as a full-time job."

It should have been a joke, but there was no lightheartedness to his words. Jillian puzzled over his remark silently as they moved at a walking pace up the uneven road, the horses picking their way carefully through the brushy growth. No simple explanation occurred to her, and some instinct prevented her from questioning Matt further. It *had* to be a joke. No rancher would toss off a remark about being a full-time guide—or a full-time anything else—except in fun. Perhaps she didn't understand the fine points of cowboy humor.

The cowboy in question certainly didn't look very humorous at the moment. He was facing grimly forward, his wide firm lips set in a straight line. Not at all the way he'd looked this morning.

There had been something bright and laughing and special about those early hours, when they had set off in the springtime of the day. She found herself imagining being a part of that life—spending long sunny days in the saddle, long autumn evenings in front of the fire, long winter nights in bed. . . .

She checked her thoughts. She was probably kidding herself, envisioning the Technicolor version of ranch life. Reality might be very different. A lot of hard work and loneliness, no doubt. Or peace and solitude and the satisfaction of a job well done. Or tired muscles and the warm companionship of someone special.

She felt a flush warm her cheeks. It was a good thing Matt couldn't read her mind. Although there were times when it seemed as though he could almost tell what she was thinking. He was looking at her now, and she quickly turned her head away, pretending an interest in the increasing noise of the unseen creek.

She said the first thing that came to mind. "The river's getting bigger."

"Or we're getting closer." He pointed to an opening in the trees up ahead.

Looking intently into the shadows, Jillian made out a dark gleam, then a brighter one. The sun shone through a gap in the trees where the road met the running water. She saw an occasional froth of white where the fast-flowing stream encountered half-submerged rocks.

"Might as well stop and let the horses have a drink," Matt suggested.

It felt strange to be on Mufrrin's back while he drank, with his head stretched down to the water instead of bobbing comfortably in front of her. Jillian rested her hands with seeming casualness on the saddle horn, then unobtrusively tightened her grip.

The stream was seven or eight feet across, swollen by melted snow, but it was scarcely knee-deep. Jillian could clearly see even the smallest stones along its rocky bed. The three horses, dappled with sunlight and shade, their muzzles buried in the water, made a peaceful contrast with the noisy energetic little creek.

As Matt signaled that the break was over, the peacefulness was shown to be only a sham. Mufrrin surged forward almost before Jillian had picked up the reins, and she was caught unprepared.

Harper was alert and waiting for Mufrrin's move. The big gray swung his hindquarters around, slamming into Mufrrin's shoulder just in front of the saddle, and knocking the lighter horse off stride. The collision sent Mufrrin splashing into the middle of the stream. Jillian felt her right foot slide out of the stirrup. Mufrrin snorted and his head snaked forward, his big teeth clamping into Harper's unprotected haunch.

Harper squealed and whirled to face his attacker. Jillian heard Matt shout. Mufrrin reared up on his hind legs, and the earth seemed to tilt beneath her. Jillian could see nothing but a brown neck blotting out the sky in front of her as Mufrrin struck at Harper with his front feet.

Jillian felt herself slipping, falling. In a split second she was out of the saddle, on Mufrrin's back and off again. The next thing she knew was the shock of frigid water closing around her as she landed full-length in the creek. It took her breath away for a second. Then she inhaled a mouthful of icy water and was suddenly thrashing and clawing her way up to the air.

Then Matt's strong arms were there, supporting her, lifting her, carrying her against his chest to dry land.

"Are you hurt? Are you hurt?" he demanded insistently while she fought to recover her breath and get her bearings.

She kept gasping from the surprise and sudden cold, but as her breathing returned to normal, her body didn't seem to be signaling any major damage.

"I think I'm all right," she said, but his arms didn't relax their iron grip. From her hair to her boots, water was streaming from her, soaking his clothes as he held her. She caught a glimpse of the horses. Mufrrin and Harper were standing well apart, rigid and unmoving, their reins trailing on the ground.

Matt's face was pale under its tan. Slowly, almost as if he were holding his breath, he lowered her and put her on her feet with infinite care, as though she might break. She straightened up gingerly. Her arms and legs all seemed to work.

"I—I'm fine." She spoke through chattering teeth. "Nothing's broken."

There was a quick scuffle behind her, a flurry of hooves. They're at it again, she thought half-hysterically. But this time the culprit was Swallow. Before they realized what was happening, the packhorse galloped past them and disappeared into the pine trees, trailing the broken end of the lead rope behind him.

"Swallow! You devil! Come back here!" Matt was shouting, but Jillian knew that it was merely an outlet for his feelings. From what he'd told her earlier, nothing could stop Swallow once he started on a beeline for home.

"I've got to get him!" Matt said decisively.

She was shocked, then frightened. "Don't leave me," she cried, clutching his arm.

He broke her grip, gently but firmly. "I haven't any choice. I have to go after him—for your sake." He turned away to snatch up Harper's reins. "I haven't any choice," he repeated. He swung into the saddle and kicked the horse into a run.

As Matt and the gray horse disappeared into the trees, Jillian stared after him. He couldn't *possibly* be leaving her here alone like this, soaking wet and half-frozen. Anger flooded her, warmed her from deep inside, then flickered out as common sense took over.

Of course he had to catch the packhorse, she told herself firmly. And everything will be under control as soon as he comes back. *If* he comes back, said a cross little portion of her mind. Of course he's coming back, she answered herself briskly. And if you do nothing but stand here debating about it, Jilly my girl, he's going to come back and find you've turned into a pillar of ice while he was gone.

Water dripped from her sodden clothes, trickled down her body in freezing rivulets. The agreeable little breeze had suddenly become an implacable enemy bent on stealing every vestige of warmth from the surface of her skin. Everything she was wearing, from her little red scarf to her Western boots, seemed to be getting colder and colder with each passing minute. She had to get out of these clothes and get dry and warm, or she was risking pneumonia.

She and Mufrrin were alone on the bank of the creek. The horse stood quietly, his reins trailing the ground. He looked composed, not at all nervous or upset. It was hard to believe that he was the battling stallion who had thrown her into the water just a few minutes ago. Still, now that she had to deal with him on her own, he looked much bigger, more intimidating, than when Matt had been here to order him around.

Jillian didn't want to approach him, but she had no choice. Her clothes felt so icelike against her body that it seemed they should be stiff. She half expected them to crackle as she moved. Uncontrollable shivers ran through her as she took a tentative step toward Mufrrin. The horse flicked his ears and watched her warily.

"I am certainly not going to say 'nice horsie' to you," Jillian told him in a quiet conversational tone of voice, talking to calm both him and herself. "Because you have just been a really naughty horse, and you know it as well as I do." Her teeth chattered a little in spite of her efforts at control. "Any self-respecting dog would have the grace to hang his head and look ashamed if he forgot himself like you just did."

Mufrrin did not look at all upset. He turned his head to watch her as she warily moved to his side and slowly reached up to grasp the leather saddlebags.

"I—I'm glad to see that you're paying attention." She was half babbling, not thinking of what she was saying, but too nervous to stop. She vividly remembered the speed and strength of his bite, Harper's squeal of pain. "I hope that this will be a lesson to you," she finished up with a little rush as she grasped the saddlebags and pulled them off his back.

She clutched them to her chest and retreated, backing up with quick short steps. Mufrrin still watched her with interest, but he remained standing placidly where he was, much to her relief.

Jillian stumbled over to a half-rotted log and sat down with the saddlebags on her knees. She started to pull out the contents, then realized that the dripping clothes she wore would get the dry ones wet. With trembling fingers she untied her scarf, stripped off the water-heavy ski jacket and the blue cotton shirt and T-shirt underneath. Her wet skin shrank from the icy touch of the mountain air. It felt colder by the minute as she tugged off her boots and socks and stood up to peel off her jeans and panties.

Bare now, and blue with cold, she dragged out her spare T-shirt and dried herself vigorously, rubbing her skin as hard as she could to restore circulation. Finally, she wrapped the damp shirt around her still-dripping hair.

Now she really could have used that long underwear Matt had advised her to bring. Instead, she had to settle for the oversize T-shirt she usually slept in. She pulled it on hurriedly, thankful that it came down halfway to her knees. On top of that she donned the long-sleeved cotton shirt and the windbreaker. That left only socks and slippers in the saddlebags, and miniscule white bikini panties almost too small to bother with. But she put them on gratefully, because every square inch of coverage was precious.

That felt better. At least the clothes themselves were dry.

But it soon became evident that they were far from enough to keep her warm.

She had fought gamely against the coldness that had enveloped her, and it had retreated. But the retreat was only partial. And brief. Now the piercing chill came stealing back, slowly but inexorably.

Jillian knew that she had to do what she could—*everything* that she could—to keep the cold at bay. She cast around for ways to help herself. Climbing over the fallen log, she tried crouching down on the other side. Yes, that put a barrier between herself and the strengthening breeze. She spread the saddlebags on the ground to make a place to sit, to insulate herself from the dampness of the forest floor.

Where was Matt? Shouldn't he be back by now? Was he still out there somewhere chasing the packhorse? And would he be able to find his way back to this anonymous spot in the trees if—*when*—he did come looking for her? She suddenly realized how big the forest was, how dark and trackless. Just a small error in direction could bring him out well above or below where she waited. And the shadows were getting noticeably longer. It felt as if the temperature were almost down to freezing already. At this altitude there might even be ice on the edge of the creek before morning came again. Jillian huddled closer against the log, her arms clasped around her knees.

What she needed right now was a nice roaring campfire. She scanned the clearing for firewood. A forest was practically nothing *but* wood, after all. There should be tons of fuel available. She saw plenty of it in every direction, but mostly it was standing tall and green and healthy, and it would take a fire storm to make it burn. The log she took shelter beside was dry, but it was far too big to serve her purpose. Here and there she could see a few fallen branches and twigs, some dead limbs. If she could just get a little fire started, maybe she could drag some of those bigger branches over to it and feed them in by their tips, slowly pushing them into the flames while they burned.

That sounded as though it ought to work. But first she'd have to build the fire. Fortunately she always carried matches. She didn't smoke, herself, but someone was always desperate for a light in the middle of a shoot. Then she'd need an armful of twigs for kindling. And some crumpled paper.

What was she going to use for paper? There was nothing made of paper in these saddlebags. Nothing at all. Except for her big black book. Jillian reached down for it. She could tear out the pages, crumple them up one by one...

No, she couldn't!

Jillian hugged it to herself tightly at the very thought. She *lived* by this book! It went everywhere she did. She could never bring herself to part with it, much less destroy it. Her entire professional life was bound up between these two covers. The telephone numbers, the contacts, the information, they were worth their weight in gold. Without this book, she'd be helpless the next time she had to dress a set or borrow a football team or produce any of the other a thousand and one rabbits she routinely pulled out of the hat for DiCicco Productions. There were not even any expendable sheets, no blank ones. She added pages, never, ever threw them away. She couldn't throw away her livelihood.

Not even to keep from dying? But it surely wouldn't come to that, she told herself uneasily. She was certainly cold; there was no denying that fact. She was shivering, shaking, teeth-chattering cold. But it was nothing *serious*. Not yet. She put the book down carefully, leaning it against the log.

There is such a thing as exposure, the logical part of her mind said sternly. And exposure had brought down more people lost in the woods than bears ever had.

But she wasn't lost in the woods, Jillian told herself fiercely. She was on a road that would eventually take her right to Mr. Alcott's lumber camp. It wasn't far away. Maybe just over the next ridge. And she absolutely refused to think one more thought about bears, because there weren't any here. And even if there were, it didn't matter, because Matt would keep her safe and he was coming back and would be here any minute now. He was definitely on his way—he *had* to be. In fact, she wouldn't be surprised if that peculiar muffled sound she was hearing right now turned out to be horses' hooves on the trail, approaching fast.

Chapter Seven

Matt and Harper came into sight, the gray horse traveling at a reckless ground-consuming pace, with Swallow laboring behind at the end of a lead rope. Jillian saw the concern on Matt's face deepen into alarm as he spotted Mufrrin standing alone by the side of the road.

"Jillian!" he shouted. *"Jillian!"*

"Over here," she answered, getting up from behind the sheltering log.

He pulled Harper to a wrenching halt that almost set the big horse on his haunches. Dismounting quickly, Matt snatched his padded vest from where he had rolled it behind the saddle and ran over to take her in his arms.

"Are you all right? You're frozen! Here, put this around you." He wrapped her in the vest. "I should have left this with you. All I could think of was that we had to have that pack. Swallow, that devil! I'll shoot him for dog meat." The words spilled out of him as though all his bottled-up fears were suddenly loosened. "You're shaking—"

"It'll be all right now." She burrowed gratefully against his chest. She was feeling the reaction, too. Some tightly wound spring inside of her seemed to let go. She shivered now because she was so cold, but no longer because of the fear and loneliness she had refused to acknowledge. After a long peaceful moment in his arms, she came back to the present enough to realize that he was still damp from when he had carried her out of the creek. "You're wet. You'd better change."

"It's okay," he said vaguely. "It's wool." He touched the fingers of one hand to the front of his shirt. "It's practically dry already." Relief seemed to have left him uncharacteristically distracted.

Jillian wondered briefly what unknown disasters he had imagined her falling prey to while he was gone.

"You're back now," she said. "And I didn't get eaten by bears. So everything's all right."

"All right?" He was looking at her clear-eyed now. "Nothing's all right. We've got to get you warm."

Matt's measuring glance took in her wet clothes draped over the log, the ragtag assortment of things she was wearing, the saddlebags she stood on.

"You did fine," he said. "You did everything you could do without a fire. Now you just wait here a minute, and we'll get you fixed up."

Jillian was reluctant to leave the warmth and reassurance of his arms, but she obediently crouched in her protected niche as he turned back to the horses.

He unloaded Swallow quickly, with no wasted motion, keeping up a running recital of bloodcurdling threats of what he was going to do to the hard-breathing horse. In a few short minutes, Matt stepped over the log with a down sleeping bag in his hands. He laid it on the ground and wrapped her in it, zipping it up. "I'll get a fire going pretty quick. I don't like that wet hair, that's not good." He brought a towel over and rubbed her hair vigorously.

Quickly, expertly, he built the fire. She huddled deep into the sleeping bag, only her eyes showing, watching him. She waited to get warm, surprised that the unrelenting chill showed no sign of loosening its grip.

He thrust a battered coffeepot into the flames. "The stuff left in the Thermos was only lukewarm. I'll heat it up in this—make fresh later."

He picked her up, sleeping bag and all, and propped her against the log. When the coffee was hot, he pressed the steaming cup into her shaking hands. He wrapped a strong warm hand around hers and helped her steady the cup enough to drink out of it.

"Mmm—that's good," she said. "I can feel it all the way down." The warmth spread through her, but only briefly. When it dissipated, she felt as cold as before.

The worried frown never left Matt's face as he sat back on his haunches and looked at her searchingly. Jillian couldn't hide the shudders that racked her body and shook the thick down bag.

"This isn't working," he said quietly. "I was so long getting back, you got too chilled to warm yourself."

He moved out of her range of vision, then returned with another sleeping bag, which he spread out on the ground. He lifted Jillian and deposited her in the center of the second bag, unzipped the first one, then proceeded to join the two together with her inside.

Jillian thought that if she couldn't warm up in a single sleeping bag, she'd do even worse in a double. But Matt worked with such swift purposefulness that she said nothing, just lay there and waited.

He sat down beside her to pull off his boots, then unbuttoned his shirt and tossed it next to her clothes on the log. Bare to the waist, he slid into the sleeping bag with her.

"Take these things off," he told her, sliding the down vest and windbreaker away from her body.

Too surprised to protest, she allowed him to turn her on her side, facing away from him, and pull her T-shirt up around her shoulders.

She started to twist a little in his grasp, but one strong hand at her midriff drew her tightly up against him, her exposed back against his bare chest, her icy skin pressed against his warmth.

"Oh," she said as she pressed herself closer, greedily absorbing his heat.

Slowly, very slowly, as the sleeping bag was suffused with the warmth of their bodies, the coldness that had claimed her began to abate. Her continuous shudders moderated into steady shivers and then to occasional ones. And finally to no shivers at all. She was warm.

Jillian's tense muscles began to relax, and she realized for the first time that she'd been holding herself rigid, trying to fight off the cold. And the fear. She could admit to herself now that she had been afraid.

But that was over. The fear and the cold and the aloneness were gone. She had never felt so safe and content as she felt here, cradled in Matt's arms.

Now that her body's need for physical warmth had been met, she was surprised to feel drowsiness begin to creep up on her. The early rising, the fresh air, the unaccustomed exercise and then the dunking, followed by the cold and fright, were all taking their toll. Her eyelids drifted shut. She opened them, blinking, then allowed them to fall closed once more. She thought she would just rest them a few minutes. She slept.

Matt felt her body grow limp under his hand. After a few more moments of stillness, he cautiously loosened his grip and let her body relax away from his. She stirred a little. He froze until her regular breathing resumed. Then he propped himself on one elbow and looked down at the purity of her sleeping profile.

A wisp of tangled blond hair lay damply across the smooth skin of her cheek, and he reached out automatically to brush it back. He stopped his hand in midair. Better leave well enough alone. He could feel sweat beaded on his forehead. He was playing with fire here.

Remember the style of life she's accustomed to, he told himself warningly. Plenty of excitement and people—interesting important people, with money to throw around. A life that offered her plenty of rewards, lots of bright lights and glitter. And money. It always seemed to come back to money.

He remembered that other blue-eyed young woman he had known at college, bright and attractive, with the prospect of a demanding career ahead of her. She wouldn't consider living at the Kemper ranch, even in the days when it was prosperous. She hadn't intended to spend her life in the "back corner of nowhere," as she called it.

He knew without conceit that he had a good mind and education, as well as a strong back. He wasn't afraid for himself. He'd make a living. There might even be another Kemper ranch, somewhere down the line. But it wouldn't come easily or quickly. There would be a lot of hard work and sacrifice involved. And that was not a prospect he could ask a woman to share with him. Any woman.

He bent a little closer to check her quiet breathing. A faint touch of color showed under the velvety skin. She was warm now, and resting. Sleep would be the best thing for her. She no longer needed the heat of his body beside her.

He eased himself out of the sleeping bag, taking care not to let in the cold air. The continued dampness of her hair worried him, and he studied the problem for a moment before turning back one corner of the sleeping bag to form a protective hood over her head.

Matt buttoned his shirt absently, his mind busy weighing alternatives. Should he leave her here sleeping and ride into the logging camp for help? It couldn't be very far away.

There was a possibility he could make it back in just an hour or so. Once they got her up to the camp, they could take her down to a hospital in Charley's truck.

On the other hand, she might wake up and panic when she found herself alone. She'd behaved pretty sensibly so far, but it was going to get dark before long. And she wouldn't know where he had gone. Perhaps he could leave her a note, wrap it around his pencil flashlight. But what did he have for writing materials? Nothing that he could think of. He sat on the log to pull on his boots and noticed Jillian's big black book lying on the ground.

He contemplated it for a moment, then slid it back into the saddlebag without looking inside. He had already decided that a note would not be called for. He was too much of an outdoorsman to ride away and leave her sleeping by an untended fire. If he put it out before he left, that would mean she would awaken in pitch-dark and find herself alone. He couldn't let that happen. Even if he went on, the chances were high that the logging camp would be deserted when he got there. That would mean no help, no truck—just another ordeal for Jillian to endure. He discarded that solution without a backward thought and turned his mind ahead to the problem of collecting an adequate supply of firewood before darkness fell.

Jillian awoke with a feeling of confusion. For a moment she didn't know where she was or how she had gotten there. She seemed to be in a small tentlike space permeated with the fragrance of wood smoke and fresh coffee. Puzzled, she pushed back the protective flap that was over her head and saw Matt sitting on his heels, cowboy-style, on the other side of the campfire. Then everything fell into place. He was staring into the fire, a worried expression on his face. She took the opportunity to lie still and take stock. She found that she was deliciously warm and ravenously hungry.

"I hope I haven't slept through dinner," she said quietly.

Matt looked over at her and smiled a little. "How do you feel?"

She stretched. "Pretty good." She moved her legs experimentally. "A little stiff. And hungry."

"Really hungry?" He sounded surprised.

"Starved. I could eat the proverbial horse." Jillian laughed. "A very appropriate remark in these circumstances. Tell Mufrrin he'd better watch out."

Matt's troubled expression returned. "Well, I brought some steaks—but I don't know, maybe you should have something lighter."

"Steak sounds wonderful. Can I help you fix it?" She sat up in the center of the double sleeping bag, and cold air flowed in all around her.

"Hey, don't get up." Matt was standing now. "Lie down and keep warm."

Jillian obeyed, for the moment. The cotton T-shirt was no barrier at all to the chill night air. "I'll be fine. I just need to get something more on."

"I rigged a clothesline." Matt gestured to a length of rope stretched between two trees. Her jeans and parka and shirt dangled heavily from it, unmoving in the brisk breeze. Even in the dark they looked wet. "But it's going to take those things a while to dry out."

"We'll just have to improvise," she said. "I can hardly eat steak lying down." She went on hastily before he could insist on cutting it up and feeding it to her, which he looked to be quite capable of doing. "There're the things I had on before. That should be enough layers to do the trick." She sat up and pulled on her cotton shirt, her windbreaker, a wool shirt of Matt's, which he had added to the pile while she was sleeping, and his down vest. She started to roll up the cuffs of the shirtsleeves so her hands would show. "There, that should take care of it. A little bulky, maybe."

Matt shook his head. "Oh, sure, that covers you up about halfway to your knees. You can't walk around barelegged like that—you'll freeze."

"My kingdom for an extra pair of jeans," Jillian said ruefully.

"Not for a horse?" Matt asked mildly.

"Right now I'd trade all three of those brutes for one pair of knee socks." She pushed the top cover back preparatory to standing up.

Matt came around the fire. "No, stay where you are. I've got an idea."

Dexterously he separated the two sleeping bags, wrapped her in one, zipped the other up halfway, and shifted her into the second one, all the while keeping her well covered. Then he finally picked her up and sat her down with her back to the fallen log, her feet and legs in the sleeping bag, pointed toward the fire.

"For a minute there I felt like the pea in a shell game," she said. "Now you see me, now you don't."

"It's important for you to keep warm," he told her. "You just stay put, and I'll take care of the cooking."

She watched him work by the light of the camp fire, admiring his swift economical movements, wishing that he looked more cheerful. She appreciated his concern for her, but the danger was over now. Tomorrow might bring Charley Alcott and a whole host of new problems, but there were a lot of things to be said for tonight. The two of them being alone together made it very special.

Later, when the fire was long out and Matt was asleep in the other bag, she gazed up at the night with a feeling of contentment that surprised her. It was hard for her to believe that she could have unquestioningly surrendered so much of her treasured self-sufficiency. All her life she had maintained a stubborn insistence on being equal to the men around her. It was so much a part of her being that whenever she had to turn to a man for help, it left a lingering trace of resentment behind.

But no matter how she examined her present feelings, she could find none of that old prickliness where Matt was concerned. Quite the contrary. The fact that he had worried about her, had been frightened for her, made her feel more content, not less.

With him so close, the dark wasn't frightening, and the sounds of the wind in the trees and the stream in its rocky bed were like friendly music. She stretched luxuriously, looking up at the stars above her. Wherever the black trees failed to blot out the sky, the stars blazed down thick and bright, large and small crowded together, shining like the promise of a million happy endings.

The only thing that was lacking was a good-night kiss or two. But there's always tomorrow, she told herself with a smile.

Chapter Eight

After a night on Matt's improvised clothesline, Jillian's clothes still hung heavy with moisture in the light of morning.

"Now what are we going to do?" she asked, dismayed.

Matt was building up the fire, getting ready to make breakfast. "I'll move them out in the sunshine once the sun gets high enough to clear the trees. Then we just wait, I guess."

"You mean just stay here and do nothing?"

He started to arrange thick slices of bacon in a black iron skillet. "I'm afraid we couldn't leave, anyway. Harper's got a stone bruise. It's not too bad, but he's favoring his left foreleg. It'll do the both of you good to lay up for a day."

"Oh." Jillian was ready to protest that she was perfectly well and had just rested enough to last her for a week. But if the horse was having problems, she could hardly argue about that. Though she wouldn't put it past Matt to invent a minor ailment just to make her more content with the interruption in their trip. She studied Harper unobtrusively for a few minutes. Yes, he did stand a little differently from the other two horses. "How did he get bruised?" she asked.

"It could have been when he was scrapping with Mufrrin. Or when we chased after Swallow. He'll be okay tomorrow."

Tomorrow, she thought. That meant they had twenty-four hours to wait before they could move on. Twenty-four hours with absolutely nothing to do. A royal inconvenience for two such busy people. Or a gift . . .

Jillian wondered which it would be as she gave her tousled hair a hasty lick with the hairbrush. "There, that will have to do until after breakfast."

Matt glanced over at her appraisingly. "I kind of like it. Reminds me of football season."

"Football?"

"You know, those big flowers the girls carry to the games. Chrysanthemums."

"Oh. Pretty shaggy even for a chrysanthemum, I'm afraid." She inhaled deeply. "Nothing in the world smells as good as frying bacon." The aroma mingled with the scent of tall pine trees and clean cold air from the mountaintops to create a perfume like no other.

Matt was surprised again at her appetite.

"I've always been a hearty eater," she said. "I'm so active that I just burn it all up."

"Are you sure that you still feel okay?" he said. "No congestion, no tiredness? You're not running a fever?" He leaned over to lay his hard palm against her cheek. She turned her face toward him slightly, and his fingertips brushed her lips as he pulled his hand away.

"I'm just fine," she assured him hastily. "Normal. Nice and cool."

"Yes," he agreed. But Jillian knew that neither one of them was quite normal now. And definitely not cool. The same thing had happened before, the unpremeditated touch that brought a heightened awareness, an electric tension between the two of them. Feelings that Matt seemed to fight each time, pushing them away with sudden anger. An anger she didn't want to see again.

Pretend that it didn't happen, she told herself. Keep it light. She summoned a quirky smile. "I'm tougher than I look. You should see me play touch football with my brothers."

He sat back silently, watching her with a half frown on his face. She propped her hand mirror on the fallen log and settled down cross-legged to tame her unruly hair. "Yes, we were five little towheads out there fighting for the ball. They didn't give an inch, and neither did I." She coaxed her hair into its usual frothy casualness and refrained from looking at him as she kept up her chatter.

Matt's frown smoothed out. "It's hard to imagine you playing any kind of football."

She gave him a quick glance that was full of mischief. "It was hard for my brothers to imagine, too. At first. One of them still calls me Red, because he says I have enough temper to be a redhead." She studied her reflection in the mirror casually. "Maybe I ought to dye it. What do you think?"

"Red would look good." His voice was agreeable, almost as light as hers. "How about green?"

"Too much trouble. I don't want to spend time worrying over blond roots." She put the hairbrush down. "There. That's the best I can do."

"It looks all right." There was exaggerated surprise in his voice. "I didn't think you'd repair that wreck short of a hundred-dollar trip to the beauty parlor."

Jillian relaxed inside. This time they had done it. This time they had backed away from the rocky path of intimacy without anger flaring up between them.

She said, "What it takes is a firm hand. Of course, it helps to have some natural curl and a good haircut."

She tidied the brush and mirror away in her makeup bag, then looked around to see what she could turn her hand to next. She had a strong suspicion that Matt was entertaining thoughts of tucking her into a sleeping bag and waiting on her all day. Jillian had no intention of lying around like some poor corset-bound creature in a Victorian novel. She felt vigorous and healthy, and all her organizational instincts were coming to the fore.

Now, what was the most important problem? What should be tackled the first of all? There was no question in her mind. Dry trousers was the number one priority. Since Matt hadn't offered to lend her a pair, she assumed that he hadn't packed any extra ones, either. What would he have done if he'd been the one to land in the creek? she wondered. He'd probably just wring them out and put them back on again. Keep a stiff upper lip. And stand close to the fire.

"I ought to be doing something about drying these jeans," she said aloud. "It'll take forever if we wait for the sun to wander in and finish the job. If I stand over there beside the fire, why couldn't I hold them up to the heat and hurry them along?"

Matt considered the idea. "Might make them smell kind of smoky," he said, but it was an observation, not an objection.

"I don't care. I'm just not cut out to play Lady Godiva. I haven't got the hair for it."

"But the rest of the equipment is more than adequate," he said solemnly, then quickly added, "I'll go haul in some more wood to keep the fire going."

He came back presently with an armload of dead branches and plans for a rack to hold the wet clothes. A tripod of short poles at each end and a longer branch across the top would allow Jillian to take advantage of the fire's heat and relieve her of the necessity of constantly holding the clothes up to it.

"Just don't turn your back on them," he warned her. "As sure as you do, they'll go up in flames."

The rack was long enough to hold her jeans and the red parka, and Jillian hung her shirt and scarf and socks at each end. She tended them all assiduously, turning and shifting each garment to the best advantage, and fed the wood into the camp fire a little at a time to keep it burning evenly.

Matt busied himself feeding and watering the horses. After a while Jillian glanced toward the fallen log and saw that he was sitting there with her boots in his hands.

"Oh, my, how did I forget about them?" Jillian exclaimed. "And I guess they'd better not go here by the fire."

Matt shook his head. "I wiped them out last night and stuffed some dry towels in them. I'll let them air out now, and probably by morning they won't be too clammy."

His words were matter-of-fact, but his gaze was steady on her, so intent that she felt suddenly self-conscious, standing there in her raggle-taggle assortment of clothes, her face all warm and flushed from the flames.

Matt was thinking that he had never seen anyone quite like her. Most women would have made plenty of fuss after yesterday's ordeal. And this morning she had washed her face in cold water and put on a dab of lipstick, and now she stood there looking so alive and vital and perfect that she put every other woman he had known in the shade. Her blue eyes were all lighted up and sparkling, and when they were turned on him, like this, he felt guiltily aware that there was another way they could handle the problem of getting her photographs, an option that he had neglected to bring to her attention.

"I've been thinking," he began slowly. "I could ride on up to the camp by myself and get you your pictures now. It would take me a couple of hours, probably. Then in the morning we'd just head back toward home."

"But what about Harper's stone bruise...?" Jillian started to protest, but the words died away as she realized that as long as she stayed behind, Matt could ride Mufrrin, or even Swallow for that matter. The idea made sense, but her first reaction was negative. She didn't want him to go without her. And it had nothing to do with not wanting to stay here by herself. She remembered vividly that Matt hadn't wanted to go into Charley Alcott's domain in the first place. If Charley happened to be in residence, and Matt rode in alone and began taking pictures, the whole scene might become rather unpleasant. With Jillian along, Matt would be escorting a tenderfoot, giving him a good reason for being there. And Mr. Alcott would have a reason for being civil. To keep everybody peaceful, she really ought to be present.

"I'd rather you waited and took me with you," she said.

"You're sure of that?"

"Yes. They might think of all kinds of questions down in Los Angeles," she improvised. "And if I haven't seen it for myself, I won't know the answers."

Later, while tending the fire and rehanging her jeans to bring the pockets closer to the heat, it occurred to her that if Matt went up there on his own, he might be able to get to the locomotive and take the pictures without being seen, even if the logging camp was occupied by Charley Alcott and his followers. But she closed her mind against the thought. She couldn't picture Matt sneaking around at anything. Integrity was his middle name. Matthew Integrity Kemper. She smiled at his back, watching him as he concentrated on maneuvering a collapsible fishing pole to drop a hook in an eddy in the stream. The smell of hot denim called her back to what she was doing. She flapped the jeans vigorously in the air to cool them.

She felt the material for the dozenth time. Dry enough, she decided. A little bit of dampness in the seams wouldn't hurt her.

It felt very good to be dressed again, to be able to tuck in her shirttail. She slid the parka along the pole, where it

would be out of harm's way, and gave herself an opportunity to step away from the fire for a change.

She tried to walk up behind Matt without making any
noise. "What are you using, a bent pin and some string?"
she asked, standing close behind him.

"Willie always leaves a little fishing tackle in the trail
box," he said, not the least startled.

"Are we supposed to be catching fish up here? I mean, is
this the fishing season?"

"Yes, it's fishing season. And I've got a license. But nobody's catching anything," Matt said comfortably. "I'm
just giving Willie's hand-tied fly a little swimming lesson."

Jillian slipped around him and sat down on the stump of
a big old tree near the water's edge. "What a beautiful
place."

Yesterday's breeze had vanished, and the air was drowsy
with warmth. The forest around them was quiet except for
the murmuring undertones of the stream. She turned her
face up to the sun. "What a beautiful day!"

"Yes," he agreed, but his eyes were on her, not their surroundings.

"This is a whole different world," she breathed, her eyes
closed to savor its specialness.

"It's not much like the city," Matt agreed.

"I suppose this doesn't seem so wonderful to you, since
you live here all the time."

"I don't live up here in the trees," he pointed out. "This
isn't my usual stamping ground. And once in a while I do
manage to get away from it all. I even went to Stanford for
four years. I'm always glad to get back, though." The ref-
erence to California seemed to trigger other not-so-happy
associations for him. "I suppose you go to Los Angeles all
the time," he said curtly.

"I've *been* there, like any other tourist," Jillian told him.
"Disneyland, and so on. I haven't been down there to work,

if that's what you mean." She opened her eyes to look up at him, standing tall above her.

"But naturally you'd like to work there?"

"Well, sure," she said, though not as positively as she might once have done. "You know," she went on, reflectively, "the first time I went to Los Angeles, it felt really weird—all the place names were so familiar. The streets—Hollywood and Vine, Rodeo Drive. La Cienaga and Mulholland. You've seen and heard about them in books and films so much that it seems as though you've already been there, or something."

"Do you know what I think of when I remember Los Angeles?" Matt stared unseeingly at the surrounding trees. "The smell of blacktop."

"Blacktop?" Jillian was puzzled.

"Yes. The hot sun on all those parking lots. The smell of heat and dust and tar."

She wrinkled her nose. "It doesn't sound like your favorite place in the whole world."

"It can't be *everybody's* favorite place." His tone was light, but he made a show of concentrating on his fishing, and she couldn't see his eyes. "If it was, all the people in the world would be there. And then it would be twice as crowded as it is now."

"Los Angeles will never be the whole world's favorite place," she said, glancing around her. "Not as long as there are spots like this one."

Afternoon sun slanted through the tree branches and dappled the sleek hides of the horses as they grazed quietly along the old logging trail.

She went on. "Even Mufrrin feels it. He seems to have declared an armistice with Harper." Mufrrin flicked his ears briefly at the sound of his name, then resumed eating.

"Nobody is challenging him for the leader's place today," Matt said practically. "As long as he is a nose in front of everyone else, he's a sweetheart. Now that we have easy

traveling on this logging road, we'll let him lead the way tomorrow.''

Jillian shivered a little. This was so idyllic a scene that she
didn't want to spoil it with thoughts of tomorrow. "Won't
Harper object if he can't be first?"

"Harp will do what he's told." Matt emphasized the
words with a flick of his wrist that dropped the fly into an
upstream pool.

Jillian fell silent, watching the motion of the bright shallow water as it flowed over the stony streambed, very conscious of his presence beside her. There was enough room
for the two of them on the tree stump, and she moved over
in unspoken invitation. After what seemed a very long time,
he eased himself down to sit next to her.

He held himself stiffly erect, keeping an inch or two of
free space between his body and hers. Jillian waited, scarcely
breathing, feeling the pull of the attraction that flowed so
strongly between them, knowing that he had to feel it, too.
After what seemed an eternity, he succumbed, slowly relaxing his rigid posture. The small gap disappeared, and their
shoulders touched.

Jillian squeezed her eyes tightly shut, blotting out her
surroundings, letting her emotions take over. The intensity
of her feelings took her by surprise. The electricity of that
simple contact was like nothing she had experienced before. When she raised her eyelids again, they felt languor-
ous and heavy.

Minutes dragged by as she waited for him to give the
slightest indication that he felt the same way she did, but
Matt remained rock still. For all she could tell, he had no
more feeling than a marble statue.

Why doesn't he just take one hand off the silly fishing
rod? she thought crossly. To all outward appearances he was
totally wrapped up in catching fish, completely unaware of
her presence.

She studied him as well as she could out of the corner of her eye, not moving her head. His hands remained quite steady, holding the rod. Nothing gave her a clue to his state of mind, until she noticed that the line had been carried into the bank downstream, and the bobbing fly was winding itself around a sprig of greenery at the water's edge.

She smiled inwardly. Whatever he was concentrating on so fiercely, it certainly wasn't fishing.

Matt stirred. "The sun's getting low," he said. "I'd better lay in some firewood for the night."

Jillian watched him silently as he followed the line down to the snag and carefully disentangled Willie's hand-tied creation. She was reassured that what she felt was not a one-way attraction. He was feeling it, too. But he was fighting it—and right now he was winning.

Matt stowed away the fishing gear and grabbed the hand ax. A man could only stand so much, he told himself as he stalked into the welcome sanctuary of the trees. All the good intentions in the world weren't going to be enough if this kept on.

For the first time he thought seriously of letting go, not just of his land, but of the whole ranching life. He could go to the city and find a job. He was accustomed to working from sunup to sundown as his own boss. He could work eight-to-five for somebody else. Wear neckties and three-piece suits. He hacked at a dead limb with the ax, working out his frustrations. Maybe Jillian could get him a job with her outfit. He could carry her bag for her. Or by the time the mortgage had run its course, he might be qualified to lecture on how to get through bankruptcy in five easy lessons. His thoughts became less coherent as the woodpile grew. He swung the ax until dusk began to gather in the trees and he had cut and trimmed enough wood to make a camp fire for giants.

Matt staggered back to the logging road with his arms piled high. When he reached the edge of the clearing, he stopped for a moment. Jillian had organized the campsite. The sleeping bags were lined up neatly side by side next to the big fallen log. She had moved the clothes-drying rack to one side and built up a hotter fire, one that was now burning down to a bed of good hot coals perfect for cooking. The smoke-blackened pot gave off fragrant odors of fresh-brewed coffee. And Jillian was squatting like an unsteady frog in the circle of firelight.

Matt dropped the load of wood on the ground. "What are you doing there?" he asked.

"I'm trying to sit on my heels like you do," she said seriously. "I can't seem to get the hang of it. There must be some kind of trick."

He smothered a smile. "I don't think there's any special trick to it," he said, his voice as serious as hers. "Probably just takes some practice. You might try it another time when you're wearing your boots. The heels might help some."

"Good idea." Jillian collapsed gratefully onto the ground. "Maybe I'll try that tomorrow." She stood up and dusted herself off briskly. "Did you work up an appetite? I'm starved."

She glanced up at him across the camp fire. Their eyes met and held for a long moment. Something leaped between them—a brightness, a promise—that brought a tentative smile to her lips and an answering one from his. A fine thread of tension spun itself between them, finally forcing her to turn away.

Watching her neat efficient movements around the fire, Matt found himself unable to sustain his previous somber mood. Pessimism gave way to a kind of recklessness born from fantasy. Perhaps a miracle would happen. Maybe he'd win the lottery. Discover oil. Rob a bank. The reality of their two different worlds seemed to disappear; those laughing blue eyes seemed to dispel all thoughts of gathering doom.

Her smile, her presence, her own sweet self—nothing else mattered. As the evening stars began to shine through the darkening sky, the whole world contracted to just this circle of firelight, just the two of them, together. The only two people in the world.

Once the utilitarian coals had served their purpose and the evening meal was over, he added fresh fuel to the fire, making the flames leap and crackle, creating an island of bright warmth in the still pool of the night.

Jillian half reclined on one of the sleeping bags, pulled close to the fire to take advantage of its heat. One last concern forced its way through Matt's newfound euphoria.

"You're sure you still feel okay?" He sat on his heels beside her, studying her face intently. Was that tinge of color under the skin from the warmth of the fire, or was it a fever flush?

"I'm perfectly fine," she insisted. "And I'm *not* running a temperature. See for yourself." She put her hand on the unruly hair at the back of his neck and pulled his cheek down against hers.

Her action overbalanced him, tipping him forward onto his knees beside her. And the touch of her smooth velvety skin against his face tipped his emotional balance, too. His arms went around her, pulling her tightly against him.

Jillian turned her face up to his as naturally as a flower turns toward the sun. Matt claimed her lips with a rough despairing urgency that paradoxically brought her back to some semblance of rational thought. There was nothing simple or casual about any of this. Not for her, not for him. She didn't understand his doubts and fears, but she knew they existed and were very real to him. She, too, had her own world. One more step along this path they were on, and both worlds could be overthrown. With no guarantee that anything could be rebuilt out of the wreckage.

Matt groaned silently. He could feel the sweat forming on his forehead. His body, his heart, all of his desires had be-

trayed him, swept away his reason. And still he could not say
the things that needed to be said. Not now. Not yet. Not
until he had come to grips with his future. Not until he could
see his way clear. . . .

Jillian knew, almost as soon as he did, that they had once
again come up against that baffling invisible barrier, the one
that said "This far and no further!" and brooked no relax-
ation of its implacable command.

Matt's strong arms still held her close to him. The sweetness of the embrace was made poignant with the certainty
that it could not endure. Their lips met again, this time in a
kiss of longing, of solemn withdrawal.

Jillian blinked away the welling tears. She closed her eyes
tightly as he laid her down gently and covered her with the
top half of the sleeping bag. That care, that tenderness,
seemed to speak volumes of love. She lay with her eyelids
rigidly shut until she heard him move away. Once he had
disappeared into the darkness, ostensibly seeing to the
horses, she got up and got ready for bed swiftly. She aligned
the sleeping bags on opposite sides of the fire, then slid into
her own and zipped it almost to the top. With little more
than the top of her head showing, she turned her face away
from the firelight. She didn't stoop so far as to pretend to be
asleep, but when he came back and damped the fire, she said
nothing. There was nothing to say.

She lay in the dark, dry-eyed, waiting for merciful sleep.
The last sight she remembered was that of the bright bitter
stars blazing down from the blackness of the sky above.

Chapter Nine

Jillian opened her eyes on grayness, a low-hanging mist that pressed down on the treetops and muffled the throaty chuckle of the stream. The damp chill made her scramble hastily into her clothes. She was grateful that her ski parka and other things were dry, though each garment was clammy and felt cold against her skin until her body heat warmed it up.

She shivered beside the camp fire. "This is like being in the middle of a cloud, isn't it?" she said, feeling shy after the events of the night before.

"That's just where we are." Matt, too, seemed ill at ease, glad to seize on a neutral topic of conversation. "It's springtime, the weather's bound to be changeable."

Jillian looked around her as they ate. Now that the sky had closed in on them, the trees seemed to crowd nearer, shrinking the small clear space even further, giving it a claustrophobic atmosphere. Or did this discomfort she felt come from the fact that what could have been a beautiful night had turned into a sullen morning, bringing uncertainty and self-consciousness?

"This mist might clear after a while," Matt said. "I hope it does. I'm not much of a forest person. I like some elbow-room, to be able to see a long way."

Was there a hidden significance in those words? Jillian wondered. Was that an oblique way of telling her that he wanted no close entanglements? Or was it just her own perverse mood making her read dark meanings into ordinary statements?

She watched Matt covertly, appreciating his easy expert movements as he broke camp, assembled Swallow's pack and lashed it tight. He saddled Mufrrin last of all and turned to help her mount.

Jillian approached the chestnut horse gingerly, remembering how large and unpredictable he had looked to her when she was alone with him. With Matt at her side, however, the horse seemed as docile as a lamb. Once she was on his back, Mufrrin moved out quietly, picking his way through the scrubby underbrush, seeming to ignore Harper at his side, though the gray horse was high stepping and fractious after a day of rest.

The road followed the creek for a while, then the stream angled away and they lost contact with it, finally lost even the sound of the fast-flowing water. The world closed down until it was only a mist-shrouded passage through tall green pines, filled with the creak of saddle leather and the muffled clop of horses' hooves.

After no more than an hour's ride, they topped a little rise and the trees ended abruptly. Jillian reined in Mufrrin instinctively, and Matt stopped by her side. They were looking down on a broad wet meadow that held a scattering of old wooden buildings, their shingles bleached gray with age.

Only one of the buildings was two stories high. Next to it stood another that was long and narrow, and, fanning out into the meadow, half a dozen small houses were scattered haphazardly. Or maybe they were shanties, or shacks. Jillian didn't know what label to put on them. Two of the smaller buildings slumped crookedly on their foundations, their moss-blackened roofs almost touching the ground. Everything in sight seemed to be a hundred years old, except for a pickup truck parked near one of the larger buildings and a silver satellite dish that eyed the gray sky from the center of the broad clearing.

"What are all the little houses for?" Jillian whispered, though there was no one abroad to hear her in the unmoving gray stillness of the morning.

"Quarters for married loggers," Matt said almost as quietly. "This place was built a long time ago. Back in the old days, it was a long trip to town from here. Sometimes a man would bring his wife with him, if the mill owner allowed it. That long building is the cook house. The big one will be the bunkhouse, and the biggest shanty is probably where Charley has been living."

The absence of movement below them and the profound silence gave the impression that the camp had been deserted for decades, that the two of them were the only humans for many miles. Except for the fact that three pencil-straight columns of smoke rose from separate chimneys to blend with the low-hanging clouds.

Jillian's heart sank. She realized how much she had counted on Charley Alcott being absent from his property. She could see the gleam of metal rails beyond the cook house, but there was no locomotive in sight—and at the moment she didn't care. She just wanted to be away from this place.

"Why three fires?" Jillian didn't care if there were two fires or twenty, but talking postponed the evil moment when they would have to move ahead.

Matt seemed in no hurry for the confrontation, either. "The cook's probably got his range going. One fire is heating the bunkhouse. And the third will be Charley's house."

"Not very democratic, is he?" said Jillian.

"The men wouldn't like it if he bunked with them."

Jillian raised her eyebrows.

"The cook will be living in one of the shacks, too," Matt explained patiently. "Cooks and bosses are a different breed of cat from the regular hired men. How are the hands going to gripe about the food and the management if everybody lives together?"

Matt twitched Harper's reins, and the gray horse moved slowly into the meadow, angling toward the largest of the shanties. Mufrrin paced alongside jealously, not waiting for any signal from Jillian. Nothing moved that she could see, no breeze ruffled the straight lines of chimney smoke. It was almost possible to believe that the inhabitants had all gone away and left their morning fires behind them.

Jillian had begun to entertain the unreasonable hope that that was the case, when the shanty door in front of them opened. A stocky man, whose thick fair hair was liberally streaked with gray, stepped onto the wooden porch and watched their approach with unwelcoming eyes.

"What the hell are you doing up here, Matt?" he demanded as the horses stopped in front of him.

"The lady needed to see you, Charley." Matt spoke in a cold flat voice Jillian had never heard before.

Charley Alcott ignored Jillian's presence, his eyes remaining riveted on Matt. "Didn't your fancy education teach you to read a No Trespassing sign when you see one?"

"You didn't make it easy to get here," Matt said in the same expressionless tone. He turned to Jillian. "Miss Curtis, this is Charley Alcott. Charley, Miss Jillian Curtis. She's come from Portland to talk some business with you."

Charley Alcott finally turned his attention to Jillian. "What business is that?" he said shortly.

"I'm pleased to meet you, Mr. Alcott." Jillian said with spirit. "I would appreciate a few minutes of your time."

"You're not in the lumber business." He made it a flat statement of fact.

"That's right. I'm not in the lumber business. I'm a production assistant for the Andrea DiCicco agency in Portland."

"And what's that?" he demanded suspiciously.

Jillian felt at a distinct disadvantage perched up on Mufrrin's back. Was he going to make her explain everything from here? "We're involved in producing television spots," she went on gamely. "Commercials, other things."

His eyes flickered to the satellite dish and back to her. "You're in the television business?"

"That's right." Jillian smiled at him, then paused deliberately, letting the silence stretch out.

"Well, if it's going to take all day, you'd better get down and come inside," he said grudgingly. He stepped down onto the wet grass to help Jillian dismount.

She stole a quick glance at Matt over the older man's shoulder. There was something uncannily similar in the two stony visages before her. Matt's face and Charley Alcott's might have been cast out of the same mold of iron-hard hostility. For the first time, she had a glimpse of what it must have cost Matt to bring her here.

Her feet on the ground once more, Jillian turned her full attention to the older man. She handed him the business card she had ready in her jacket pocket. He read it, gave her a quick sharp glance and studied it again. Then he stepped back and opened the shanty door. Jillian followed him inside, making a determined effort not to look back at Matt for support.

The interior of the shanty was cluttered but comfortable. Four easy chairs faced the television set. Jillian perched on the edge of the nearest one. She explained, as concisely as she could, that there was a possibility that a movie might be shot in the area and that the company might be interested in renting his locomotive for the film.

Charley Alcott looked down at her with suspicious eyes. "How did you get my nephew to bring you up here?" he asked when she had finished.

"Your *nephew*?"

Charley Alcott inclined his head toward the door. "Yes," he said flatly, "my nephew."

Jillian's first reaction was complete disbelief. It wasn't possible that Matt had brought her up here to see his own uncle without saying a word about the relationship. Could he be that closemouthed? Why would he do such a thing? Of course! Matt was one of those who blamed Charley Alcott's locomotive for setting the fires last year. And Charley Alcott denied it and refused to accept any of the responsibility. Her heart sank. She had apparently blundered into what was not only a community quarrel, but a family feud, as well.

Charley Alcott was looking her up and down speculatively. "I'm surprised that there's anything at all that could get Matt to come up here without an invitation." His voice was heavy with innuendo.

Jillian stiffened. "Matt did try to talk me out of it," she said crisply. "He convinced me that the road was impassable for a car. So I knew I had to get up by some other means. I—"

"What other means?" he interrupted.

"I thought...a trail bike." She gave him a steely look that dared him to doubt her.

He shook his head. "You wouldn't have made it."

"Perhaps not," she said. "But it was my job to try. I need to send photographs of your locomotive to the producer in Los Angeles before he can make a decision—"

"How'd you get hold of my nephew in the first place?" Charley Alcott brushed aside her talk of moving pictures and Los Angeles.

"I didn't know that he was related to you."

"Matt never mentioned it, eh? Well, I suppose he wouldn't." Charley Alcott straddled a straight chair and studied her searchingly. "So how *did* he get mixed up in this?"

Jillian chose her words with care. "I met him when I was taking photographs of the Kemper house."

Charley absorbed this information thoughtfully. "So your movie outfit is interested in Matt's place, too. That right?"

"DiCicco Productions is only doing the preliminary scouting for a large film company." She made her voice as businesslike as possible. "We'll give them a variety of locations, and they'll pick out the ones that meet their requirements. *If* they decide to come to this part of the country at all," she added warningly.

Charley frowned in deep concentration. "Still, Matt must figure he's got the inside track, or wild horses couldn't have dragged him up here."

"All I do is take pictures, Mr. Alcott," she said quietly. "I have no part in the final decisions. Matt understands that."

The older man looked her up and down again with a deliberateness that fanned a spark of anger in her. "Maybe Matt figures he's got an inside track somewhere else."

"This is a business proposition, nothing more." Jillian kept her voice level with great effort. "The film company would pay you well for the use of your locomotive. *If* they're convinced that it would fit their purposes."

"They pay good money, do they?"

Jillian felt tempted to promise him the riches of the Indies, anything to terminate this disagreeable interview. "As I said before, I have no authority to make promises. I do think you would be satisfied with the price. Always providing—"

"Providing they decide they want it," he finished for her. "I understand that."

He studied her with hooded eyes. Jillian realized that he was no longer seeing her, that his attention had turned inward, to some private calculations he was making in his own mind. She could almost feel the seconds as they dragged by in the stillness of the room, and she felt an urge to go on talking to dispel that silence. But something held her back, warning her to let him work it out for himself. He was dealing with considerations that she had no power to address—such as his relations with his neighbors and with Matt.

When his eyes focused on her once more, he seemed to have arrived at a decision. "All *you* want is your snapshots? Is that right?" he asked.

Jillian nodded silently, afraid that an incautious word might quench this spark of reasonableness.

"Well, I guess there's no harm in that." Charley Alcott got to his feet. "The engine's up the track, by the log deck. I'll drive you up there in the truck."

She would have greatly preferred to finish the ride as she had begun—on Mufrrin, with Matt beside her. It was on the tip of her tongue to turn down the proffered ride...diplomatically, of course. To tell him that she didn't want to impose on him, shouldn't take up his time, something like that. But she realized how big a mistake that would be. He naturally wanted to be the one to do the honors in his own territory. To suggest that Matt escort her around *his* logging camp would be untactful, to say the least. "Thank you, I'd appreciate a ride," she said. "I'll just have to get my camera first."

"That's okay. I'll go over and get the truck."

Matt and the horses were waiting outside just as she had left them. Matt looked unseeingly off into the distance and ignored Charley Alcott as the older man walked away toward the cookhouse.

"I need the camera out of the saddlebags," Jillian told Matt. "Your uncle has offered to drive me up to see the locomotive." She emphasized the word "uncle," letting Matt know that she had learned of the relationship and was just a little bit cross that he hadn't warned her in advance.

Matt seemed oblivious. He found the camera and handed it down to her. "He's cooperating, is he?"

Jillian looked after the stiff retreating back doubtfully. "I think so. He hasn't said whether he'd be willing to rent to us, but at least he's going to let me take some pictures."

The locomotive looked even more impressive than Jillian had expected, bigger and blacker, a mass of cold iron. It was shining with moisture now that the morning's mist had turned into a fine cold drizzle. Jillian had a momentary urge to climb up into the cab and play engineer, but, of course, that wouldn't have been businesslike.

Charley Alcott patted the wet metal affectionately, as though it were alive. "What do you think of her?" he asked as Jillian aimed her camera and snapped her pictures.

"It looks pretty impressive to me," she responded. "I'm sure that the film company will take wonderful care of it, if they decide to use the locomotive in the movie. They'll even get it repaired for you," she added.

He shot her a swift angry look. "Who says it needs repairing?"

"I mean..." She was aware that she had blundered. "You know, all that talk about ... about ..."

"The fires last year," he finished the sentence for her. "There was nothing wrong with this engine then, and there's nothing wrong with it now."

Jillian was silent. Maybe he even believed that. Or maybe he just wanted to believe it. In spite of the evidence to the contrary.

Charley Alcott went on, "No matter what anybody says, there never was one thing to link my spur line with any fires. After the second fire, I had an expert up here to go over this locomotive with a fine-tooth comb. And he gave her a clean bill of health."

"He did?" Jillian couldn't keep a slight trace of disbelief out of her voice.

"Sure he did. I've got the certificate at the house. I'll show it to you when we get back."

"But nobody even *mentioned* that. Not a word." Now she was indignant for him. "How could everybody just ignore that kind of evidence?"

"I didn't show it around," said Charley Alcott.

"You didn't show them!" She stared at him with mounting exasperation. That was carrying stiff-necked pride a little too far. "Why ever not?"

"It was all after the fact," he said flatly. "Didn't prove a thing. I could have had her repaired in a hurry and *then* imported the inspector to check her over. That's what they would have said in town. No, I had him up here for my own satisfaction. I know the responsibility doesn't lie here."

Jillian looked unseeingly at the piled logs beside the track, her brows knitted in thought. "And yet the train went by and the fires flared up behind it," she said almost meditatively.

"Just because one things happens and then another thing happens, doesn't mean that the first thing was the cause of the second one," he pointed out. "The rooster crows and then the sun comes up, but the rooster doesn't make it happen."

"But it must mean that someone wanted to put you out of business," Jillian said, excitement lighting her face. "They wanted to keep you from hauling your logs to the mill. And once you stopped, there wasn't any need to set any more fires."

"Or you can argue it just the other way around," he pointed out. "And that's what everybody did. They believed the fires stopped because the train wasn't running anymore to set them off. I just said the hell with all of them."

Jillian recalled Matt telling her of Charley's stubborn refusal to accept any blame. "Matt told me that you claimed all along that somebody set those fires."

"I didn't just 'claim' it," he said. "I *knew* it. What I could never do was prove it."

"It was somebody who wanted to put you out of business," she suggested.

He shook his head. "Oh, I thought of that. But I never came up with anyone who fit the bill. The lumber business was so slow back then that I was practically out of business, anyway. I was already thinking of laying off for the winter. This just closed me down a little quicker—and tighter—than would have happened otherwise."

"People don't do something dangerous like setting fires without a reason," Jillian said positively.

"Some people are crazy enough to do anything."

She brushed that idea aside. "If it was just craziness, then no one might ever figure it out. But if there's a *reason* behind it, then there should be some kind of indication of who was responsible. Who benefits? Or who loses? That kind of thing. If the fires weren't directed at you, then what about the fields that burned? Who owned them? What was in them that was destroyed?"

Charley Alcott gazed down at her indulgently. She knew that look only too well. She could almost read his mind. He was thinking that she was being naive and childish, but kind of cute, too. Insisting on sinking her baby teeth into his big adult mystery, worrying at it like a terrier puppy. But what she was saying made a lot of sense, she was sure of it.

"Well, let me think, now." His voice was indulgent, too, but at least he was trying to answer her question. "The first fire took out Matt's wheat, and—"

"Matt's wheat was burned?" she interjected.

"Didn't he mention it?" Charley Alcott shook his head. "No, he probably wouldn't. Yep, it burned out a nice stand of grain, just ready to harvest."

So Matt had been a victim of the fires. No wonder bitterness had made a wall between the two men. Charley Alcott had lost the respect of the community—and of his closest relative. Matt had lost a crop of wheat he needed badly.

"Matt's been having hard row to hoe," Charley Alcott was saying, "and losing that harvest made it worse for him. But I don't see where it did anybody else any good. The second fire was on Smithfield land, and it burned up some good grazing. But nobody sold up or moved out on account of either one."

"There must be a connection somewhere," Jillian insisted.

"Don't you think I haven't pondered over that, sitting up here all winter watching the trees grow?" He shook his head again. "But there's no point in you worrying your head about it. People have already made up their minds about what happened. They aren't going to change now."

From the bleak expression on his face, Jillian could guess that he was talking about Matt.

"You're getting wet," he said. "You'd better get back in the truck."

Jillian took one last picture, then she complied. There was no denying that it was more comfortable to be inside where it was dry.

Charley Alcott started the engine and switched on the heater. "I suppose you're planning on riding horseback through these wet woods to get home."

She nodded briefly. "There's no other way to get down, since the road is blocked." She closed her mind to an unwelcome image of herself and Mufrrin forcing their way through unyielding pine branches now sodden with rainwater.

"I'm thinking I might open up that road." Charley Alcott drove slowly back the way they had come. "I can send the crew out to clear the way and take you back to town in the truck.''

Jillian's first reaction was one of dismay, and her first thought was to discover some inoffensive excuse for declining his handsome invitation. The truth was that she wanted to stay with Matt. Never mind the weather. She wasn't made of sugar; she wouldn't melt.

On the other hand, how could she turn down an offer to open the road? That was an enormous concession on his part. To refuse it would surely give further insult to an already embittered man.

She didn't know what to say, so she said nothing. He seemed to take it for granted that her silence meant consent. They drove into the clearing around the logging camp, and Jillian saw that Matt had taken the horses and withdrawn to the edge of the trees.

Charley Alcott stopped in front of his shanty and left the engine running while he went inside to bring out the certificate he insisted on showing her.

Jillian forced herself to concentrate on the official wording of the locomotive's bill of health. ''No defects,'' the engineer had written.

''Just seven days too late, so it's not proof. And there's no way now of ever getting any proof,'' Charley Alcott said when she handed it back to him. ''I suppose you've got some of your gear over on those horses. You go collect what you need, and I'll start the crew on ahead of us.''

The truck jounced across the trackless meadow and stopped just long enough to let her slide out into the cold freshness of the rain, then pulled away in the direction of the bunkhouse.

Matt drew her into the shelter of the overhanging branches. ''Is everything all right?'' He was wearing a bright yellow slicker. Another one just like it was draped over Mufrrin's back, keeping the saddle dry for her.

Jillian had an unreasoning impulse to burrow into his arms, to have him hold her tight and let her close her mind to any more difficult decisions. Instead she said, "Your uncle offered to drive me back to town. He's sending some men down to clear the road."

"Charley's going to open the road?" Matt looked very surprised. And pleased. "He'll drive you down? That's great, Jillian."

Jillian could have done with a little less enthusiasm. Was he so glad to get rid of her? she wondered. "I don't know about that," she said. "I feel like—like I'm running out on you, leaving you here in the rain."

He shook his head at her, smiling. "Oh, I'm used to this. But I certainly don't want to see you getting all soaked and frozen again. This way you won't have to take another chance on catching pneumonia."

She felt a familiar impatience. "I wish you wouldn't act as though I'm liable to break."

"I know," he said, but his relief was still obvious. "I know. But look at it this way. We'll both get home a lot quicker and easier if you ride with Charley."

An engine started up behind them, somewhere out of sight. Jillian turned to see a different truck, a larger one, drive out from behind the bunkhouse and disappear into the trees.

"There goes the road crew." Matt felt as though a weight had been lifted from his shoulders. He turned to the horses. "You'll want to take your things with you."

He slid the saddlebags from Mufrrin's back and stood holding them, looking down at her, wondering why she should have that wounded-doe look in her eyes. Riding down the mountain in the rain with Charley might not be exactly a picnic in the park for her, but it certainly would solve their immediate problem. It would get her back to civilization warm and dry. And it would get both of them off Charley's property as quickly as possible.

He thought that he must not have been in his right mind when he'd first agreed to this expedition. He'd been thinking about those sunny blue eyes, not about the raw humiliation of presenting himself in this place where he wasn't wanted and wasn't welcome. Jillian wouldn't understand his feelings, of course. There was no reason why she should. But he wished that she wouldn't look so forlorn. He wasn't really abandoning her by sending her off ahead of him; he was just taking care of her the best he knew how.

"Where shall I meet you in Enterprise?" he asked her.

"In Enterprise?" she echoed. "Why can't I wait by the first roadblock? I could stay in your truck until you come."

Matt shook his head. "You might have a long wait before I catch up with you. Charley wouldn't want to leave you there alone. And I agree with him, for once."

"It might take them all day to clear away those roadblocks," she protested. "You could be right behind us."

"And I could be hours behind. Those fellows are good loggers." He wondered why she was being so unreasonable. "I wouldn't put it past Charley to have things rigged so he could clear that road pretty slick, anytime he took the notion."

He couldn't stand that sorrowful look. He wanted to take her in his arms and tell her that he'd *walk* her home if that would make her happy. But they had to be sensible here, and sensible meant a nice dry ride in Charley's truck for Jillian.

"You go on into town," he said. He had a sudden flash of inspiration. "Get yourself a nice room at the Wilderness Inn. Have a good hot bath. When I get home, I'll pack up your things and bring them in, and we'll go out and have dinner."

Her eyes changed, and the sadness disappeared. That's

better, he thought. Now if Charley would just hurry up they could all get a move on, get themselves out of this damnable spot they were in.

Chapter Ten

The truck moved down the road slowly, giving the crew up ahead time to do their job of clearing the way. The drizzle had steadied into a cold rain, not heavy but sullenly persistent. Jillian scarcely recognized the world that she and Matt had ridden through on that golden morning only two days before.

She studied Charley Alcott's profile covertly as he drove. Now that she knew he was Matt's uncle, it was easy to see the resemblance. No wonder she had felt that the two of them looked alike in their stubborn pride. And they acted alike, too. If Matt had been shown that inspector's certificate, it would surely have made a difference in his attitude toward his uncle. Or had things gone too far by then? There had certainly been a great outcry over a couple of accidental fires.

"The first fire," she said tentatively, "did it make a lot of trouble for Matt?"

Charley Alcott answered slowly. "The Kemper ranch has been in trouble for nearly ten years. Ever since Tom Kemper went into debt to buy the old Skinner place."

"Skinner?" Jillian asked. "You mean Hob Skinner?"

He nodded. "Cattlemen," he said reflectively. "None of them ever think enough is enough when it comes to buying land. It's a disease that's ruined more ranchers than hoof-and-mouth. Tom Kemper was riding high back then. Didn't owe a cent. And prices were so good he figured to turn a hundred-dollar profit on every animal he sold. That was when Hob Skinner decided to sell up and go live in town. Beef prices were high, but land was higher, and interest rates were the highest of all. Hob held up Matt's dad for every cent he could squeeze out of him. Tom Kemper paid too much for the Skinner place, and then he died and left the debt to Matt. And the good prices didn't last. Matt's seen years when he *lost* twenty-five dollars on every cow he sold. It cost more to raise them than he could get for them."

"I don't understand," Jillian said. "Hob Skinner was talking to me a few days ago—he was trying to find out what I was doing at Matt's house—and he said that pretty soon the Kemper ranch was going to belong to *him*."

"Hob said that? That don't make sense."

"I thought the same thing. He lives like he hasn't a cent in the world."

Charley Alcott frowned speculatively. "Hob hasn't spent any noticeable money for quite a while, that's for sure. If he took everything he got for his place and socked it all into the bank back then, grabbed some of that sky-high interest, he could have more than doubled it by now."

"Frankly, he didn't look that clever to me."

"No, it's hard to think of Hob as smart. I can see him as miserly, though. I always figured he got cold feet when it came to spending anything and ended up just sitting on that money. I remember he talked about waiting for just the right investment to come along."

The truck slowed to a crawl as he turned his head to look at Jillian.

She saw her own concern reflected in his eyes. "Can Hob Skinner be telling the truth? Is Matt really losing the ranch?"

Charley Alcott shook his head slowly. "I'm not sure. If he'd only come and told me—"

"But that's just what Matt couldn't do, not after all the hard feelings!"

He went on as though thinking aloud. "Something could have been arranged. Maybe an extension on the loan. Beef prices are starting on the way up. It's beginning to make sense to be in the cattle business again. All he needs is to hang on a while longer."

Anger swept through Jillian like a flame. "Don't you see? It was Hob! He burned Matt's wheat. Because he's after the ranch!"

"I'd like to think it was Hob." Charley Alcott spoke softly. "But is he bright enough to figure out a long-range scheme like that?"

"I hardly know the man," Jillian answered, remembering the little trick that had netted Hob her business card. "But I've found out that he's sly, and quick to take advantage of an opportunity. He might have known that Matt was on the edge, and that losing his crop would help to push him over. And while Hob was out there thinking about setting the fire, he could have seen the train go by. And he took a chance on shifting the blame in your direction. Was Hob one of the concerned citizens who spoke up against you?"

"Hob was the loudest."

"Not Matt?"

"Matt goes quiet when he gets mad. He didn't say much at all. He didn't listen much, either," Charley Alcott said grimly. "Not to me, anyway."

"But he'll *have* to listen now!" Jillian looked back the way they had come, wishing Matt would appear so she could tell him what she'd discovered.

"People hear what they make up their minds to hear," Charley Alcott responded. "We've come up with a theory, that's all. You won't convince Matt without some kind of real evidence."

"But you've got your certificate." Jillian knew she was on the right track. "And Hob benefits. He's the only one who does benefit. He managed to drive a wedge between the two of you so you wouldn't be offering to help Matt. And Matt wouldn't be asking you."

"Matt still wouldn't accept anything from me, if I know him at all."

"We'll just have to tell him and see."

"He wouldn't listen before." The older man's voice was flat. "I'm not going to ask him to reconsider at this late date." They were passing the spot where the highest road-block had forced Matt and Jillian to take to the woods. There was nothing to be seen of it now but broken pine branches littering the road. The trees had been tipped over the cliff.

Jillian was exasperated at Charley Alcott's attitude. Maybe they couldn't actually *prove* what had happened, but surely Matt was entitled to hear who his real friends were— and his real enemies. It was a good thing that she was around; somebody had to let him know. Tonight at dinner she would clear up this silly misunderstanding. The truck was starting to travel a little faster now, which suited her mood. She couldn't wait to see Matt's face when she told him.

"Where are you staying in Enterprise?" Charley asked after a few minutes' silence.

"The Wilderness Inn," she answered absently. "But my car's in a shed at Matt's place. And some of my things are still in the house."

His hands tightened on the wheel. "I guess that's for you and Matt to straighten out. I don't go places where I'm not welcome."

"I understand." Jillian saw that further argument would be futile. She had some other arrangements of her own to make, she realized. After nearly breaking her neck to get snapshots of that elusive locomotive, she had quite forgotten about them in the midst of these revelations. At the rate they were traveling, she would arrive in town too late to send the pictures to Andrea today. Even another expensive charter flight wouldn't get them to Portland in time to make the overnight mail. How *could* she have forgotten? Those pictures were what this trip was all about. She should be itching to sling her things into the Porsche and hit the road for home.

Instead, she could only think of all the reasons why leaving was impossible.

She stole another look at her companion. There was definitely no way to persuade him to stop at the ranch, she thought. And, even if he would, Matt had padlocked the shed, and she didn't know where the key was kept. And probably Willy wasn't home, either, and she wouldn't be able to get into the house. In short, she didn't want to leave. What she wanted was to go to the motel and have a lovely hot bath and put on her blue jersey dress and have dinner with Matt.

Just ahead she saw the lower roadblock; the men were still at work clearing away the trees. Matt's truck and the horse trailer waited on the other side of the barrier. How wonderfully convenient it would be if Matt should come into sight right now. But it didn't happen.

On the ride into town, Jillian chatted to Charley Alcott on neutral subjects. But he wasn't fooled about where her true interests lay. "You're still determined you're going to tell Matt all that stuff, aren't you?" he asked, pulling up beside the Wilderness Inn.

"He has a right to know."

"Well." There was a world of doubt in the single sylla-ble. "I'll likely stay with someone here in town for a couple nights." He caught the surprise she was unable to hide. "Oh, yes, I still got a friend or two left around here. I'll call your motel and leave you a number, in case you need to get in touch with me."

Once she was installed in her second-floor room at the motel, Jillian indulged herself in a long steamy bath. The hot water soothed her saddle-weary muscles. It felt deli-cious to be so clean, so relaxed—and so elated about what she had to tell Matt when she saw him tonight. In spite of the clouds that still lingered after the morning's rain, the whole world seemed as bright as a new-minted coin.

Once all this misunderstanding was cleared up, Matt would have no more worry about losing the ranch. His uncle could help him to get the loan extended, or something. Charley Alcott hadn't actually pledged to do that, not in so many words, but Jillian had no doubt that he would. Char-ley *had* to intervene, if only to see that Hob Skinner didn't profit from his actions.

She pulled on her trail-soiled jeans one more time, not even minding, because she knew she had a dressy evening coming up in just a few hours. She was buttoning her shirt when the telephone rang. She padded across the rug bare-foot to answer it, expecting the caller to be Matt.

"I've been phoning you for two days," Andrea said. "Did you get the rest of the pictures?"

"I just got back with them," Jillian answered. "*And* the road is now open, so if someone from Los Angeles wants to have a look, he won't have to wander around the woods on a horse, like I've been doing."

"I was expecting you in Portland yesterday."

"Well, we ran into a little trouble, and—"

"Trouble?" Andrea cut in sharply. "What kind of trouble?"

"Nothing to worry about," Jillian soothed her. "I fell into a stream and got wet, and we had to stay in camp for a day to dry out."

Andrea was silent for a few seconds. "Well, aren't you the sly one." Her voice was amused, almost admiring. "I didn't think you had it in you. I take it that we'll have complete cooperation from Mr. Kemper from now on."

She might have known that Andrea would leap to the wrong conclusion. "It was nothing like that," Jillian said levelly. "And I don't see any point in going into all this on the telephone."

"There's one thing more," Andrea went on. "I took a call for you this morning. From Enterprise. It was some man who wanted to know if you work for DiCicco Productions."

Jillian was puzzled. Who would be calling her from Enterprise? "Did he leave his name?"

"Let me see, I have it somewhere. Here it is. Skinner. Hobson Skinner."

Jillian clutched the telephone receiver more tightly. "Hob Skinner? What did he want?"

"So you do know him, then." Andrea's voice turned censorious. "What in the world are you doing over there? Broadcasting our business from the street corners? I thought I could depend on you to do a quick discreet job. To pop in and pop out. Not spread the news all over town."

"I'd like to see *anyone* just 'pop in' on Charley Alcott when he had the road barricaded," Jillian replied with spirit. "And as for Hob Skinner...I didn't tell him a thing. Not one word. How much did he learn from *you* when he called?"

"Well, naturally I thought he was someone else you'd taken into your confidence, since he had this number to go along with your name."

"What exactly did you say to him?" Jillian persisted.

"He asked for you, and I told him you weren't here. And then he demanded to know if you worked here. I said that you did. I didn't care for the tone of his voice. He seemed to think that I was some little receptionist he could bully."

That sounded like Hob, all right, Jillian thought. "And then I suppose he wanted to know what kind of a business DiCicco Productions is."

"He seemed to think he already knew. Where did he get the idea that we have something to do with real estate?" Andrea sounded offended.

"Did you tell him the truth?" Jillian asked.

"It was obvious by then that he was simply fishing for information. I suggested he leave his number if he wanted you to call him when you got back into town. Then he had the nerve to quiz me about where you were, if you really weren't in Portland. Because there was no sign of you around Enterprise, and you weren't staying at any of the motels."

"I hope you hung up on him."

"Yes, I did give myself that satisfaction," Andrea said. "Do you know what he was after? And how did you get involved with someone like that in the first place?"

"He seems to have some wild idea that he's going to buy the Kemper ranch. He got the telephone number by knocking over my purse and helping himself to one of my business cards. But he knows absolutely nothing about this movie deal."

"Well, I hope he doesn't find out." Andrea sounded decidedly unhopeful. "The kind of work we do isn't exactly a secret. If he knows anyone else in Portland, all they'd have to do is look in the yellow pages. The information is there to find, if he is persistent enough."

Jillian felt a momentary unease. She was sure that Hob was quite capable of digging until he got some satisfaction. Not that it would do him the least bit of good, now that she was about to heal the rift he had caused between Matt and his uncle. "There's a long involved story behind all this," she said slowly. "I'll fill you in on everything when I get into town tomorrow. Expect me about noon."

"Why tomorrow? If you've got the pictures, you can start back right now. Time is money, Jillian. And I need my car. I'm sick of taking taxis."

"I have to wait for Matt to bring some of my things from the ranch," Jillian told her.

"You left some things behind?" Andrea sounded amused again. "Well, just thank him nicely for his trouble, and then come on home."

"I'm having dinner with him tonight."

"Can't you try to get out of it?"

"I have no intention of trying to get out of it." Jillian let her annoyance show.

"Well, maybe you're right," Andrea conceded. "We don't want to spoil our public relations, do we? Not when we've got things on such a friendly footing."

"Goodbye, Andrea." Jillian put the receiver into its cradle with exaggerated care. It was the only way she could stop herself from slamming it down.

By the time she had her temper under control, the telephone rang again. This time it was Charlie Alcott, leaving her a number where he could be reached. Jillian was anxious to keep the line free for Matt's call, so she kept the conversation brief. The wait seemed long, but finally the phone rang a third time. It was Matt.

"I just got back to the house." The sound of his voice served to recharge her anticipation of the evening to come. "I see all your stuff is still here. Just what I expected. It would have been a surprise if Charley had let himself set foot on any property of mine."

"That's right. I'm sorry, but—"

"Don't worry, I'll take care of it," he assured her. "I'll just pack it up and bring it in with me."

"The car is the problem," she said. "I'm here, and it's there."

"I forgot that you'd be worried about that car." His voice was noticeably cooler. "I'll work something out. I'll get it back to you without a scratch."

Jillian was annoyed with herself for getting sidetracked onto the dreary subject of Andrea's Porsche. That wasn't what she wanted to talk to Matt about at all. "I wish I'd never taken Andrea's stupid car!" she burst out. "I could have rented something perfectly adequate, but no, nothing would do but she had to pack me off in the Porsche because it was fast, fast, fast! As though a few miles per hour made that much difference."

"*Andrea's* car?" Matt interjected when she stopped for breath.

"Yes, Andrea's car. Andrea's pride and joy. Andrea's status symbol—"

"Not *your* car?"

"No, of course not," she said. "My car's an old Volkswagen van that's on its last legs. But it's a lot more useful than that silly Porsche," she added.

"Well, don't bother your head about it. About anything." Matt sounded suddenly cheerful. "Leave it to me. I'll arrange something."

When Jillian opened the door at Matt's knock, it was as if she were greeting a stranger. Dark gray slacks, gray plaid sport jacket, a white shirt and maroon silk tie seemed to transform him into a young stockbroker or an up-and-coming executive.

She stood rooted in the doorway for a minute before stepping back to let him in. Yes, it was the same Matt. The same endearing shaggy hair that stirred such protective feelings inside her. The same intense blue eyes. And the same smile. No, not the same smile. This one was wider, more free somehow.

"You look gorgeous," she said.

His smile got even wider. "I think that's supposed to be my line."

She glanced down at her rumpled jeans and shirt. "I'm afraid it's not appropriate right now. Maybe you could save it for later." She gestured toward the small suitcase and shoulder bag he was carrying. "I'm certainly glad to see those. This is the first time I ever registered in a motel with saddlebags for luggage."

He deposited her things on the Indian-patterned bedspread. Jillian opened up the bag and rummaged inside for her little jersey dress. She went into the bathroom to change, taking the suitcase with her. Nylons, heels, blue button earrings to match the dress. Thank goodness jersey didn't wrinkle. She did her makeup quickly, expertly, and put the finishing touches on the artless froth of her hair. And all the while she could hear Matt walking around the close confines of the other room, as though something was making him feel too keyed up to sit down.

When she came out, she saw the look in his eyes that she had been hoping to find. Admiration. Appreciation. And just a tiny bit of surprise. He hadn't seen her in evening eye shadow and four-inch heels before.

There was something else in his expression, too. Something that she couldn't quite put her finger on.

"Now you look gorgeous," he said. "No—" he paused to choose his words "—more gorgeous." He shook his head, still unsatisfied. "Just different gorgeous. There was nothing ungorgeous in the way you looked before."

She smiled up at him, thinking that there was definitely a change in Matt. Gallant compliments had hardly been his style before.

In the parking lot, she saw his truck and Andrea's car parked side by side, and turned to him, with raised eyebrows.

"Willy drove the pickup," he said. "He's got a sister i[n] town. I'll find him when it's time to go home." He took out his keys and turned to unlock the truck, then stopped as a new thought struck him. "Maybe you'd rather we took the car."

Jillian slanted an unenthusiastic glance at the Porsche then turned an assessing eye on him. He read her thoughts as clearly as if she had spoken them aloud. She was wondering if *he* would prefer another opportunity to be in the driver's seat with all that powerful machinery. Her blue eyes clouded ever so briefly, then cleared. She shook her head decisively. "I'm tired of sticking out like a sore thumb," she said. "I'd just as soon blend in." She stepped up into the dusty truck with a brief flash of silken legs, leaving a faint breath of perfume behind her.

As he turned onto the main street, Matt said in a deliberately nonchalant voice, "You know, I thought that red car belonged to you."

"To me! You thought it was *mine*!" Jillian started to laugh, then stopped abruptly. "Well, that certainly must have given you some wrong ideas about me."

"It certainly looks that way." He caught her eye, and they both laughed, a spontaneous irrepressible laughter that neither one could quite keep under control during the short drive. Laughter that threatened to break out afresh even after they were seated at a table in the corner of the sparsely filled restaurant.

He watched her over the top of the menu, savoring that feeling of unfamiliar merriment inside himself. He wanted to laugh out loud, not because anything was so humorous but because everything was so different, so *special* now. No[t] everything, his soberer side reminded him, but he pushed the thought aside. "Tell me about yourself. I want to know al[l] about you."

That topic and others kept them engrossed throughout the leisurely meal. They talked and talked while their steak[s] grew cool on their platters and their ice cream softened in the fluted dishes.

He had never seen her so alive, so full of brightness and smiles. Her eyes danced, as though she was hugging a delicious secret to herself. When she looked at him over the candle flame, he ventured to believe that some of her delight was because of him.

Finally, as she stirred her coffee, she fell silent for a moment, her eyes no longer seeing him as she focused on a thought she was trying to put into words. "Matt," she said tentatively.

"Yes?" He bent closer to hear her better.

"About your uncle..."

He put out his hand to cover hers. "Never mind Charley. Forget him for tonight."

"This is important, Matt. I've got something to tell you."

"Something important?" A cold finger of premonition touched him. "What is it, then?"

"On the ride down from the logging camp, your uncle and I had a long time to talk...." She looked at him with a slight frown. "Matt—" the words spilled out suddenly "—what would you think if I told you that the community was mistaken, that his train had nothing to do with those fires last year?"

The disappointment hit him like a blow. Matt straightened and pulled his hand away from hers. The feeling of specialness went out of the evening, and anger flooded in to take its place. "What would I think?" He let his bitterness speak for him. "I'd think that Charley must have given you an ultimatum, told you to choose between renting his locomotive or my ranch house. And ranch houses being a lot more plentiful than railroads around here, I guess I shouldn't be surprised if you figure you have to go over to Charley's side."

An answering anger leaped into her eyes. They blazed at him as she crumpled her napkin in one hand and flung it on the table. He expected her to stand up and stalk out of the restaurant. For a long moment she sat so still she might have been a marble statue—if marble were capable of exuding fury from every pore.

Jillian clenched both fists on the tabletop and leaned toward him. In a tone of utmost scorn, she said, "That is absolutely the *dumbest* thing I've ever heard!"

The utter conviction in her voice carried its own verification. Matt had the sinking feeling that he had just made a disastrous mistake.

Chapter Eleven

Jillian stared at Matt hotly for a minute, then her first flash of anger began to abate a little. She should have taken into account that getting Matt to see that his uncle was in the right was going to mean making him accept that he was in the wrong—and had been from the beginning. No wonder his initial reaction had been denial. No matter how pleasant the final outcome might be, some masculine pride was going to be sacrificed along the way.

"All right, then." Matt was stiff lipped. "What am I supposed to think?"

Under that bleak gaze, her evidence seemed thin and unsubstantial. She squared her shoulders and presented it defiantly. "For one thing," she said, "your uncle had the locomotive inspected, and there was nothing wrong with it. He has a certificate that says so."

Matt's face was unreadable. "When was this?"

"Just a week after the fires."

"*After* the fires?"

"Yes," she admitted. "After. But he didn't have any reason to get it done before."

"He could have got the thing fixed and then had it inspected," Matt pointed out.

"He could have. But he says he didn't. And I believe him." Jillian spoke even more positively than she felt.

"It seems as though he might have mentioned that before now." Matt's expression was noncommittal, but his voice was milder than it had been.

Jillian had to acknowledge the truth of what he said. "He thought that nobody would believe it."

"Charley might have saved some of this fuss if he'd given the rest of us a chance to hear his side of things." Matt went on thoughtfully. "He has plenty of faults, but lying isn't usually one of them."

"He didn't think it would do any good. And he didn't want to stand up and try to defend himself if the rest of the people were just going to hoot him down. It would have been different if he could have offered them an alternative explanation of what caused the fires. But he didn't have one then."

Matt went very still. "And now he has?"

"*We* have," Jillian said enthusiastically. "Charley and I figured out that the fires were deliberately set!"

He shook his head, his disappointment plain. "Sorry, Jillian. There was never any evidence to back that idea. And no one's going to find any at this late date."

She leaned forward. "Because you're supposed to look for someone who had the means, motive and opportunity—and nobody seemed to have a motive. That was the most important question—who benefits? Well, now we know who benefits." She took a deep breath, preparing for Matt's disbelief. "Hob Skinner."

"Hob Skinner," Matt said softly.

Jillian started to explain the tortuous thread of reasoning that had led her to that conclusion, but stopped when she saw that it was unnecessary. Matt's expression told her that he could work it out for himself, now that he had accepted the possibility that his uncle might not be at fault. "Hob Skinner," he repeated.

"You believe that he did it!" To Jillian's surprise, what she had begun as a question came out as a statement of fact. Matt's nod confirmed it.

"Anyone who knows Hob could believe it," he said. "We had him next to us for a dozen years, and he was never what you'd call a good neighbor. Funny things would happen to our fences, and our blooded bulls would find their way to Hob's old scrub cows. Things like that."

Jillian could hardly believe that it had been so easy. Aside from Matt's first disagreeable outburst, of course. She had been prepared for an extended argument, and now all opposition seemed to have vanished like smoke in the wind. "Isn't it wonderful?" she exclaimed. "This changes everything!"

Matt looked at her quizzically. "What does it change?"

Jillian felt her own eagerness turning into impatience. Couldn't he *see*? Was he going to make her say it in so many words? Now that he and his uncle had no quarrel with each other, Matt could ask Charley for his help. For a loan. Or to guarantee the loan that the bank already held. Just enough to save the property he'd worked his heart out for all these years.

Studying him now, she could tell just by his expression that he was not about to ask any favors of Charley Alcott. In fact, she had the staggering conviction that the situation was even worse now. It was still every bit as impossible for him to ask his uncle for help as it ever had been. Even Jillian's fertile imagination couldn't picture Matt going to the older man and saying, "Hi, Charley. It kind of looks like I've been wrong about you all these months. So how about lending me some money?" From what she knew of Matt, that was just about the way he would look at the situation.

But it wasn't fair! And it wasn't right, either. They couldn't just hand Hob Skinner everything he'd schemed for. "Are you going to let Hob go ahead and profit by what he's done?" she demanded. "Aren't you going to do something?"

He smiled grimly. "What would you suggest?"

"Well..."

He made a fist of his right hand and struck it lightly into his other palm. "I could beat him up." He nodded thoughtfully. "He'll sue me, of course. Hob is great for lawsuits. But what have I got to lose that Hob's not going to get already?"

"You're not serious!" Jillian searched his face for some indication that he was joking.

His eyes were unreadable. "I'm not sure. Maybe I am serious. At least when the judge asks me why I did it, I'll be able to say in a court that Hob Skinner committed arson. Right now it looks like that's the only way I'll ever get the chance."

"Well, it wouldn't be worth going to jail for," she said, alarmed. "If the two of us put our heads together, we should be able to come up with something more satisfactory than that."

"We?" he said, and smiled.

It was exactly the wrong kind of smile, the kind she couldn't tolerate. The patronizing smile she refused to take from anyone. The kind of smile that said, "Don't bother your pretty head, little girl, we men will take care of this."

Sure, they would take care of it, Jillian thought wrathfully. The adult males would go at each other with fists and clubs and ruin everything, rather than listen to a little feminine common sense. If Matt could look at her like that, then maybe she had almost made the biggest mistake of her life, thinking that he was special. Believing that what they had between them was special.

As she sat in furious silence, his smile gradually faded. Once again he looked like the person she thought she knew.

"Do you have any suggestions?" he asked quietly.

She studied him, her suspicions not quite allayed. Was he just humoring her? He did seem to be sincere. She decided to give him the benefit of the doubt. "We should figure out just what it is we need to stop Hob, then go out and get it."

"About the only thing that would really nail him at this late date is an eyewitness," Matt said. "If anyone had seen him out in the field with a lighted match, they would have come forward last year. There's no use hoping that kind of evidence will turn up now. So what we need is a confession from Hob."

"Then that's what we have to go after." Jillian tried to sound more hopeful than she felt.

"So you're saying that I should beat him up, after all," Matt said.

She gave him a withering look. "I certainly am not! We'll have to trick him into confessing, somehow." She admitted to herself that their chances of success were very slim. She said aloud, "He's bound to be on his guard with you. But with me—"

His hand closed over hers again. "You're not having anything more to do with Hob. He can be a very mean customer."

She looked down at his hand, so firm and warm on her own. Then she looked into his eyes, their expression tender and protective. In a perfectly even voice, she asked, "Do you honestly believe that I'm some useless fragile female who has to be taken care of every minute of her life?" She was disappointed in him. And angry. Much more angry than she had been when he'd accused her of taking Charley's side to secure the use of his locomotive. Those words had been blurted out in the heat of the moment. But this—this was apparently his true opinion of her.

Matt flushed darkly and removed his hand. "I apologize," he said harshly.

Jillian held his eyes with hers. "All this may seem trivial to you, but it happens to be important to me."

After a moment his expression softened. "I really am sorry."

After a pause, she said, "Could we come to an arrangement? Whenever I need help, I'll yell for it. But until I do..." She let her voice trail off.

"I'll try. It won't be easy. But I'll try."

No, it wouldn't be easy, Jillian thought philosophically. It wouldn't be easy for either of them. She would have to make some allowances on her side, too. After all, he was a strong silent Western type. Letting her stand on her own two feet would probably go against all his training and every instinct he possessed. But she believed that now he understood just how she felt about her own independence. It remained to be seen whether he could respect those feelings.

Matt said, "But I'm still not agreeing to having you square off with Hob Skinner all on your own."

She sighed inwardly. So much for equality. Then she told herself to be fair. There was something to be said for Matt's point of view. She mustn't let pride stampede her into foolishness. Did she really think that she could handle Hob Skinner if she did actually get him cornered?

"Maybe we could work out some kind of a compromise," he offered. "If you're sure you want to try talking to Hob, you could do it where there are other people around. In a public place. A restaurant, for instance. And only if I'm on hand, in case he starts to make trouble."

Jillian nodded slowly. "That sounds reasonable." She looked up at him. "Let's do it."

"It's a deal."

Jillian felt encouraged by Matt's acceptance of the idea that she could be involved. She leaned toward him eagerly.

"I've been thinking about what you said earlier—that no witness ever came forward. Do you think we could make Hob believe that someone was there, that someone did see him?"

"Convince him that there was a witness?" Matt considered the idea. "That would be a good trick, if there was any way to pull it off. It might rattle him. Or he might just laugh."

"We'll have to work on it, find a way to make it convincing, somehow." She paused to organize her thoughts. "I could tell him I'm a private investigator," she said brightly.

"It says something different on your business card," Matt pointed out, half smiling at the idea of Jillian as a gumshoe. "Don't forget that Hob has seen it."

She frowned. "Private investigators probably use phony business cards all the time," she said after a moment.

"I guess that's believable," Matt said. "So okay, you're going to be a private detective. And you're going to talk to Hob. Then we need a place for our showdown. How about the restaurant across from the courthouse?" She nodded agreement, and he went on. "That's settled, then. You'll be there—and I'll be there. Now if we can just get *Hob* there, we'll be in business."

"I could call and ask him to meet me, I suppose. He's eaten up with curiosity about what is going on. He even phoned Andrea in Portland and tried to pump her for information." She shook her head doubtfully. "For me to call him just doesn't feel right."

"It would put him on his guard," Matt agreed. "And our only chance is to take him by surprise, get him to admit something while he's too shocked to know what he's saying." Privately he felt that their chances of pinning anything on Hob were practically nonexistent, no matter how they went about it. But he kept that to himself. "I think we have to let him call you."

"He doesn't even know I'm back in town."

"No, I suppose he doesn't." Matt thought it over for a moment. "But if he could catch a glimpse of the Porsche, that would do the job. If I were Hob, and I saw that red car go by, I'd soon track down which motel you were staying at."

Jillian smiled. "That's brilliant! All I'll have to do is drive around the streets for a while. The first thing in the morning—" She broke off, giving Matt a stricken look.

"What's the matter?" he asked, concerned.

"Andrea's pictures! I forgot all about them. I'm supposed to get them to her by noon tomorrow!"

She saw, mirrored in his eyes, the realization that had already come to her: if she went away now, when would she get the chance to return? A week? A month? Or the movie might never get made, and she'd have no opportunity at all.

She put her hands to her face. She was *not* going to leave the next morning. She refused to go away with this problem unresolved between Matt and his uncle, with Hob Skinner ready to rake in the fruits of his wrongdoing.

Jillian looked across the table at Matt. "Those pictures *have* to be there in time to catch the overnight mail."

"You agreed that you'd yell for help if you needed it," he reminded her.

"Well, you can consider this an SOS," she said, though she didn't see what he could do, what anyone could do.

"Let's figure something out. The immediate problem is getting those pictures to Portland. As long as they get there, you don't necessarily have to deliver them in person. I'll find someone to take them. Maybe one of Willy's nephews would make the trip to Portland, if he gets paid for his gas."

"And I can call Andrea in the morning and tell her to look for him," she said. It occurred to her that that was not going to be an easy explanation to make.

In truth, Jillian wasn't sure that she quite understood what was happening herself. Any other time she would be dashing back to Portland as though heading for a four-

alarm fire, triumphantly delivering those hard-to-get snapshots. When had the wonderful exciting possibility of
working on an honest-to-goodness movie receded into the
background of her consciousness? When had she begun
thinking of the photographs as *Andrea's* pictures?

She had better get back to reality, get her mind back on
her job, the job that she loved. The one she did very well. As
delightful as life on the ranch might be in fantasy, she still
had a strong doubt that Matt could ever accept her for the
kind of person she really was.

The next morning Jillian ate her breakfast in a small restaurant near the motel. Neither she nor Matt had said it in
so many words, but they both realized that after their leng-
thy dinner in the evening, he could hardly come in to have
breakfast with her. In a town of two thousand inhabitants,
it would be an open invitation to scandal.

The snapshots were already well on their way to Portland; one of Willy's sister's brood had hit the road with
them before sunrise. Matt had made the arrangements after leaving her at her motel room door last night.

He had kissed her good-night. In deference to the pro-
prieties, it was a rather brief unsatisfactory embrace. "I'll
be here the first thing in the morning," he had said huskily.

That had sounded lovely to her. But she had forced herself to stop and think whether that would be the best thing
for their plan—their poor feeble one-chance-in-a-million
plan.

"Wait," she'd said. Even that brief kiss had left her
slightly breathless. She had pushed that interesting realization out of her mind to concentrate on the more immediate
problem.

"Should we be together," she'd asked, "when I drive
around town to let Hob see the Porsche?"

Matt had been silent for a moment, obviously thinking
the same thing she was. In order for this to work, it was

better to give Hob Skinner the impression that theirs was a
business arrangement, not a personal one. "Suppose we
leave it that I'll be at the ranch until I hear from you. The
minute Hob gets in touch, you call me. And we'll plan our
strategy from there."

Now Jillian was pushing her scrambled eggs around her
plate with her fork and thinking uncomfortably that some
clever strategy was just what she needed. This situation
called for an actress, not a production assistant. Someone
able to tell huge lies while looking the other person straight
in the eye and making them believe every word. Something
she had no talent for at all. Big lies, little lies, her eyes gave
her away every time. As the star of this upcoming scene, she
had some serious shortcomings. She would need all the help
she could get from wardrobe and props.

She had already decided that Hob Skinner would never
take her seriously if she wore her blue jeans. Her jersey dress
and white blazer would have to do. She glanced down at
them critically, thinking that a plain dark suit and a trench
coat were what she needed.

She paid her check and went out to drive slowly around
the not-very-numerous streets of Enterprise. At first, it
seemed to her much too obvious to turn down the little road
to nowhere that went by Hob Skinner's house, but then she
reconsidered. Why not? What could she lose? She drove
past the ramshackle house slowly, went on for a quarter of
a mile, then found a spot to turn around and drove back
again. After that she headed back to the motel, prepared for
a long wait for the fish to rise to the bait. Give him an hour,
she told herself. No, make it two hours. Maybe three.

The telephone rang as she walked in the door.

"This is Hob Skinner," a voice announced when she answered.

"Yes?" Jillian replied noncommittally, not sure she was
ready for this.

"I've been trying to get hold of you," he went on.

"You have?" She kept her voice cool.

"You're back in town," he said accusingly, as though she might attempt to deny it. "And you had yourself a long talk with Matt Kemper in the restaurant last night."

So much for their clever plans to attract his attention. He'd probably been trying to get her on the telephone all the time she was parading around. She hadn't reckoned on the speed with which news could travel in a small town.

"I want to talk to you," Hob continued in a hectoring tone of voice.

"All right," she said, still very cool.

Her easy acquiescence seemed to take him by surprise. He fumbled for a second before replying. "I know where you're at. I'll be right over."

"No," Jillian told him quickly. "Not here. I—I have other appointments this morning. I can pencil you in for... let me see... one-thirty this afternoon. I'll meet you at the little restaurant across from the courthouse."

"Here and now is good enough for me—"

"One-thirty," she told him curtly. And hung up.

Now she had to get away from here quickly, in case Hob refused to wait and came pounding on her door. She and Matt had arrangements to make.

She made one hurried call to tell Matt that contact had been made. Then she was on her way. She had a queasy feeling that the confrontational machinery they had set into motion was threatening to run away with her. She needed some time to get properly settled at the wheel and fasten her seat belt. Butterflies fluttered in her stomach, and she hadn't even come face-to-face with Hob Skinner yet.

Matt was watching for her at the ranch. He came out to meet her and had her leave the car in the shed again, just in case Hob showed up to scout the area.

He put his hand on her shoulder protectively as they walked slowly to the house. Jillian drew reassurance from his strength and nearness, and the butterflies quieted.

"How's it going?" he asked.

"Almost too well." Jillian tried to keep her voice light. "I was busy worrying that our fish wouldn't notice the lure, and the first thing I knew he was trying to jump into the boat with me."

He nodded, not happily. "Hob's a real shark. A little shark who would like to be a big one."

Jillian's antennae went up, searching for the first hint that he was about to change his mind, back out of their agreement, forbid her to keep the appointment with Hob.

He opened the kitchen door for her. She walked in, dropped her shoulder bag on the checkered tablecloth and turned—straight into his waiting arms.

At first she felt a faint surprise at her own willingness to draw on his strength, to set aside her own treasured independence, but the pleasure of his warm embrace soon banished all thought. Her body molded to his, as though she had become liquid. She felt his heartbeat, echoed it with her own. She was aware of his hard masculinity as never before.

Jillian's hands moved up the strong column of his neck, her fingers slid into the thick shagginess of his hair, and she pulled his mouth down to hers.

Matt kissed her softly, with a gentleness that first tantalized, then quickened her desire. He raised his head to look down at her with unreadable eyes before claiming her lips again, this time with fierce hunger, as though a single kiss was not enough, would never be enough.

Jillian closed her eyes, closed her thoughts to everything but this enchanted closeness, this delicious surrender of the senses.

It was Matt who finally stirred, breaking the spell. "Are you all right?" he asked her. "Are you sure you still want to go through with this?"

"Of course I am," she said, answering both questions at once, trying to make her voice sound nonchalant. She looked up at him with a reassuring smile, but her eyes wavered under his gaze. Her heart sank. If she couldn't carry off just a tiny white lie to Matt, how was she going to make Hob believe a whole fistful of whoppers? If only she could hide her too-revealing face. She turned away.

"I know!" she said suddenly. She reached for her bag and tipped out its contents onto the tablecloth. She poked around in the heap. "Here's what I need." She slid her sunglasses out of their case and put them on. The kitchen turned darkly mysterious, and Jillian felt a little darkly mysterious herself. The sunglasses gave her the sense of security she had been looking for. Behind their impenetrable barricade, she would go and prevaricate the socks off Hob Skinner.

Matt cocked a considering eye at her. "You look like you're going to meet him in the middle of Main Street at high noon."

"I told him to come to the restaurant at one-thirty. I didn't feel that I was quite ready to face him yet. Maybe I could even be a little bit late. It wouldn't hurt to give Hob some time to sit and worry."

Without conscious thought, her mind busy on other things, she found cups and saucers and poured coffee for the two of them. It was as though this kitchen was her natural habitat, as though she belonged right here.

Silence fell between them. Matt drank his coffee mechanically, then brooded over his empty cup. Finally, he looked over at her somberly. "Remember, even if Hob does happen to admit something today, all he has to do is deny it later on. It would be your word against his. Anyone who knows Hob would rather believe you than him, but legally it still wouldn't count."

"I know." Jillian traced one of the red squares of the tablecloth pattern with her fingertip. "We need a judge and jury hiding under a chair."

"Or maybe a tape recorder," Matt suggested.

Her face lighted up. "I've got one! It's in my bag some-where." She sorted through her possessions, spilling every-thing out in a jumbled heap on the table again. "Here it is."

Matt's worried frown softened as he looked at her. "Is the kitchen sink in there, too?"

"Look, I'll put it here, on top of everything else, and I''ll turn it on just before I go in. If he lets one little word slip, we'll have him!"

"We'll have something to convince our friends," Matt said. "But secret tape recordings don't hold up in a court of law. That doesn't matter. None of this really concerns the law."

"Maybe not. But it does concern what's right and what's wrong." She lifted her coffee cup in a mock toast. "To justice."

Matt found himself unable to respond to her gesture. He was desperately worried that she was in for a crushing dis-appointment. Jillian setting out to beard Hob Skinner with her little sunglasses and tape recorder was like a popgun going up against a Sherman tank. All Hob had to do was keep his mouth shut, and he was impregnable. Seeing the look of expectation in her eyes now made Matt feel even worse, because he would soon have to stand by and see it quenched. He didn't want her to learn that a brave heart doesn't always bring victory.

Matt's arms ached to shelter her, to hold her close and keep her from this imminent disaster. He wanted to tell her the meeting was off, to forget about the whole thing. But he was in no position to issue any such commands. He was sure that if he tried, she would be more than disappointed—she would be disappointed in *him*.

It was a small comfort that he would be on the spot, ready to step in if the situation took a turn for the worse.

"If there's any justice at all," he said, "I'll at least get the chance for one good punch."

A tiny frown appeared between Jillian's eyebrows. "You're planning to come inside the restaurant? Hob will see you."

"Let him," Matt said firmly. The very least he could do was be there. He had no intention of lurking around on the street somewhere while she was face-to-face with Hob Skinner.

"Well, I guess that will be all right," she said after a doubtful pause. "I plan to tell him that I'm working for you, anyway. You and your uncle. Together." Her blue eyes studied him warily. "But at the beginning, I'm going to go inside alone," she added.

He could see that she was ready to challenge him if he objected. He nodded a cautious agreement. He wouldn't be far behind.

"I'll get him to sit near the back, facing away from the door," she said thoughtfully. "Then he might not notice you at first." Her lips quirked. "I'll stroll right past him and take the seat that's most advantageous for me. Since he wants to talk to me, he'll just have to come where I am."

"That's the spirit," he said with forced enthusiasm. "Shall we synchronize our watches?"

Her eyes lighted up as she smiled.

All at once, that smile, that bright confidence, seemed more precious than anything in the world. Matt realized that he would give everything he had to keep her from unhappiness. He didn't have much, but he could think of one more thing that he could throw into the pot.

His pride.

When the time came for her to leave, he saw her off with the assurance that he would be close behind. As soon as she disappeared down the road, he sprinted for the house—and the telephone.

Matt knew where in town his uncle was likely to be staying. When a feminine voice answered, he cleared his throat and asked for Charley Alcott.

"Yes?" Charley asked harshly.

"Charley, this is Matt."

There was an unforgiving silence on the other end, but Matt had expected nothing else. He spoke bluntly. "Meet me outside the restaurant across from the courthouse at one-thirty."

"Matt?" His uncle's voice boomed down the wire, full of anger and surprise. "What the hell are you talking about?"

"Jillian—Miss Curtis—and I are going to be there, and Hob Skinner, too. She's going to try to trick Hob into admitting the truth about those range fires."

"You must be crazy!"

"I know. But Jillian won't be satisfied until she tries. She won't have a chance unless the two of us are there to back her story—"

"You've got no business letting that little girl get mixed up in any of Hob Skinner's messes."

"I know that! Better than you do."

"It'll never work."

"It *won't* work if we waste time arguing on the phone. Jillian needs some way to shake up Hob, and the sight of the two of us walking in acting like ordinary civilized human beings might be enough to do it." Matt waited tensely for his uncle's reply.

"All right, I'll meet you." Charley Alcott's voice was as hard as before. "And I'll expect a damn good explanation when I get there."

Chapter Twelve

Jillian took a deep breath, adjusted her sunglasses and pushed open the door of the small café. Head up, her walk brisk and confident, she swept past a surprised Hob Skinner and seated herself in the farthest booth of the nearly empty restaurant. She felt a faintly hysterical impulse to laugh at the expression on his face when she passed him by. It was an impulse that died quickly as he left his table in the middle of the room and slid in opposite her.

"What's the matter?" he demanded. "Can't you tell who I am with your dark glasses on?"

"Of course I recognized you, Mr. Skinner." Jillian was gratified that her voice worked smoothly in spite of the nervous quivers inside her. She told herself to handle this situation as Andrea would. Practical, businesslike, unsentimental. She gave Hob Skinner a severe look. "Even though we are in a public place, we can endeavor to make this a private conversation. Unless you have a preference for broadcasting your business?"

"This is okay," he said grudgingly.

Jillian plunged ahead, trying to keep the initiative. "I understand that you have already discovered that DiCicco Productions is not a real estate concern. Is that correct?"

"Some snippy girl in your office laughed at me." Hob was vindictive. "You ought to fire her. I could have been a customer."

"I hardly think so, Mr. Skinner. You aren't likely to be in the market for an investigator, are you?"

His eyes sharpened. "It says DiCicco *Productions* on the card."

This was going to be a tricky part. Jillian tried to sound offhand. "What we 'produce' for our clients happens to be information. Reports. We investigate, gather facts—"

Hob was not easily deflected. "If you're investigators, then why doesn't it say Investigations?"

She took refuge in her most superior tone of voice. "Because we are not that kind of a firm, Mr. Skinner. Discretion is what we sell. And perseverance. We're not ordinary private investigators—"

"You're a private investigator?" Hob's washed-out gray eyes narrowed. "Let me see your license!"

Where did he learn that? Jillian thought, alarmed. Her mind worked swiftly, cataloging everything in her purse that might possibly be passed off as a detective's license and would be convincing enough for a quick glimpse across the table. But she couldn't count on that, either. Hob would surely grab it from her and scrutinize every word. Her library card definitely would not do.

She said, "You've been watching too much TV, Mr. Skinner." She gave him a reproving look, hoping that her brief hesitation hadn't been noticeable. "I am not required to produce a license when I am neither interviewing you nor seeking information. You might remember that this meeting is entirely at your request. If you want to terminate it, that's fine with me." She held her breath, hoping that this mishmash of nonsense would overwhelm his objections.

"What do you think you're investigating, then?" he asked with rude insolence.

Jillian raised her eyebrows haughtily, then remembered that the dark glasses rendered that gesture ineffective. "I'm investigating the fires." She held her breath for his reaction.

"You're a little late, aren't you?"

He didn't ask which fires she was talking about, she noted, feeling her first little twinge of satisfaction. He knew well enough. She felt more confident as she served up her next lie. "We've been on the job longer than you think, Mr. Skinner. We've had you under observation for quite some time."

He gave a bark of disbelieving laughter. "You haven't seen much, then."

Her eyes flickered involuntarily toward the entrance to the restaurant. She had expected Matt to put in an appearance before this. She was using up her meager store of ammunition at a frightening rate, and she couldn't see that she had made the slightest dent in Hob Skinner's confidence.

"We've seen more than you think," she improvised, trying to sound completely assured, even a little bored. "We are entirely satisfied." She abandoned her elegantly languid tones for a little plain speaking. "We were just waiting for the rat to finally stick his head up out of the slime—and you obliged us a few days ago."

Hob flinched as if a pet bunny rabbit had suddenly taken a bite out of him. "You're a *crazy* woman!" he said with complete conviction.

She shook her head as though disappointed in him. "You announced your guilt the day you let it be known that you were after the Kemper ranch."

"Hey, my money is legal! I can account for every penny!"

"Nobody is accusing you of being a thief, Mr. Skinner." Jillian gave him a pitying smile.

"You'd better not! And you'd better not accuse me of anything else, either!" He brought his voice under control with an effort. "What is it you're after, anyway?"

"We're after the man who set the fires, Mr. Skinner." Jillian nerved herself to fire her big guns, tell her big lies. "You set them. You were seen."

His eyes stared into hers as though he could see through her dark glasses. "Nobody saw me setting any fires," he said defiantly.

"Not precisely in the act, I'll grant you that." She had the scary feeling that she was losing ground. "But you have been placed suspiciously close. At the operative time, shall we say..."

"Who says?" Hob demanded. "There isn't any person who saw any such thing. If there was, he'd have come forward long before this."

"You can hardly expect me to tell you his name here and now. According to the law, you'll be entitled to full disclosure once the district attorney decides to bring the case to court. Not before." Too bad it wasn't Andrea sitting here in her place, Jillian thought. Someone with size and forcefulness was needed to put over this shaky story. "We were waiting to establish the motive for the fires. You've wrapped it up nicely. Means, motive and opportunity."

Hob showed no sign of being intimidated. "I never heard such a load of hogwash."

She went on, a little desperately now. "Last fall you realized that the entire Kemper ranch might be within your grasp. There's your motive. You were seen near the scene of the fire at the significant time, so you obviously had the opportunity. As for the means...well, anyone can come by a match easily enough."

"They didn't find any burned matches in either of those fields," Hob said confidently.

Jillian seized on that tiny morsel of encouragement. "You seem extremely sure of what they did or did not find, Mr. Skinner."

"I read the papers," he said shortly.

"The authorities never make public *everything* they discover in criminal cases. And that holds true in fire investigations, as well."

"They still never found any burned matches," Hob repeated stubbornly. "And you're not much of an investigator if you're under the impression that they did."

Jillian tapped her fingernails on the tabletop, then made herself stop in case he interpreted it as nervousness. "I think I should make a note of the fact that the subject shows unexplained knowledge of the evidence found at the crime scene."

He gave her a mirthless grin. "In that case, you better write it down as evidence *not* found. Because there isn't any such evidence. And never will be. This case will never see a court."

"That decision is entirely up to the authorities. I'm referring to the criminal case, of course." Jillian felt that she was chattering. She didn't know any longer whether she was making sense or not. *Where was Matt?* "Naturally," she went on quickly, "the civil case is another matter entirely. Mr. Kemper and Mr. Alcott can bring suit against you at their own discretion. For crop damages. Lost revenue from the logging operation. Defamation of character—"

Hob Skinner laughed at her. "Matt Kemper and Charley Alcott get together long enough to sue me? That'll be the day!"

At that moment the outside door opened, and Matt strode into the restaurant. Jillian's eyes went to him gratefully, while he did a masterful job of pretending not to notice her from a dozen yards away. He's a better actor than I am, she thought a little giddily.

Matt pulled out a chair at the same table where Hob had been sitting when she came in. For the first time, her gaze slid past Matt to the person who had entered just behind him. Charley Alcott sat down opposite his nephew and signaled to the waitress. Then he leaned forward casually and said something to Matt.

The sunglasses apparently hadn't concealed from Hob that he had lost Jillian's attention, and he turned his head to follow the direction of her gaze. Then he jerked back in his seat as though he had received a physical blow.

Jillian realized that Hob had just seen his dream shrivel and die. And at the same moment, she saw her own dream blossom. Charley Alcott at Matt's side. Charley Alcott talking conversationally, Matt nodding in agreement. The gray head and the fair untidy one close together in amiable discussion. The one person in the world who might buy Matt enough time to get back on his feet was sitting right there beside him, chatting as though nothing had ever been wrong between them.

She had to hit the demoralized Hob while he was vulnerable. "As you can see," she said, "there never was any real estrangement between Mr. Kemper and Mr. Alcott. It was merely part of the plan." She pressed him mercilessly. "You won't be left with a dime of your precious money once they bring suit against you." She made a motion as though preparing to leave. Hob reached out and grasped her arm.

"It wasn't like you think," he bleated. "That first fire was practically an accident."

She brushed his hand away contemptuously. "I suppose you just happened to be there when the train went by, and the wheat was so ripe and ready that the lighter just jumped into your hand."

His eyes were glassy. "It wasn't like that. I never planned to do it! I didn't—"

Jillian could see the shock wearing off. She leaned forward tensely, willing him to go on.

His expression sharpened. "I didn't set no fires!" He recovered quickly. "Nobody can prove I did any such thing." He cast another glance in Charley Alcott's direction. "Nobody's going to take my money away."

"We'll see about that in court, Mr. Skinner." Jillian felt such a heady sense of triumph that for a moment she believed her own words. "Personally, I don't think much of your chances. Especially now that you've just confessed to me that you are the guilty party."

Hob's face went hard. "I did no such thing."

"I heard you say it, Mr. Skinner."

"You heard nothing," he snapped. "Because I said nothing. You swear I did, I'll swear I didn't. No jury will believe I told you a thing like that. Not when I knew you were working for *them*." He jerked his head in the direction of Matt and his uncle. "You keep your mouth shut, or I'll get you hauled up for perjury."

Jillian snatched off her sunglasses. The man was completely vile. "No one will need to take my word for anything," she said rashly. "Because this conversation is all on tape!" She raised the recorder just far enough so that Hob could see it over the edge of the table.

His eyes darted sideways like a trapped animal's, then came back to the tape recorder, unwillingly fascinated. "You can't record me," he whispered. "That's not legal."

"We'll see what's legal." Jillian spoke more quietly, too. She was beginning to regret her impulse. Hob was right—the tape would be inadmissible as legal evidence. "That's for a judge to decide."

"You can't record me without my say-so and then use it against me," Hob said, still keeping his eyes on the recorder. "So what's your game? The three of you. You want money. Is that it?"

"Don't judge everyone by yourself," Jillian said with profound disgust. "We don't go in for blackmail."

"Blackmail! That's what this is—they're trying to blackmail me," Hob said rapidly, directing his words to the machine in her hand. "There, now you got the real truth on that illegal tape of yours!" His eyes flickered to her face, showing a glimmer of triumph that quickly died. "But those things can be tampered with—maybe you can cut that part out." He caught his breath raggedly, then seemed to take hold of himself. "It's a blackmail scheme, and it isn't going to work. That tape doesn't mean a thing, because you can't use it in court. You're not getting a cent out of me."

"All I want out of you is a little justice." Jillian's anger ran away with her again. "There's such a thing as the court of public opinion. How many people will have to listen to this tape before the news will be all over town? It will only take one or two. And how will you like *that*, Mr. Skinner?"

Hob raised himself up in his seat, and his hand darted out like a striking snake. Her fingers tightened around the tape recorder, but his hand closed over hers with crushing force. He slid out of the booth and got to his feet, dragging her with him. She was unable to resist his wiry strength, and pain shot up her arm as he twisted it.

"Matt! Help!" she called out.

Matt loomed up at Hob's shoulder before the words left her mouth. With one hand he spun the older man around. His right fist struck Hob in the midsection, a short savage blow that knocked the air and the fight out of Hob and stretched him gasping on the restaurant floor.

"Are you all right?" Matt asked Jillian.

She nodded, flexing her tingling fingers. "I'm all in one piece." She looked around quickly for the precious tape recorder, bent down and scooped it off the floor.

When she straightened again, Charley Alcott was glowering at Matt forbiddingly.

"You shouldn't have hit him like that, Matt," he said balefully. "A man as old as Hob. You should have let me hit him."

"I'm sorry, Charley." Matt's voice held no apology. "You can have the next shot at him, as soon as he gets up."

Hob Skinner sprawled on his back, his head resting against the side of the booth. He was making no move to regain his feet. He looked up at them with hate-filled eyes. "This won't do you a bit of good," he told Matt.

Matt returned his gaze coldly. "Let's just say it was a million dollars' worth of satisfaction," he answered.

Hob sneered. "You can't take satisfaction to the bank."

"Don't be too sure about that, Hob," Charley Alcott interjected. He turned to Jillian, who was standing in the circle of Matt's protective arm. "I expect you got what you came for, or Hob wouldn't have lost his head like that."

Jillian nodded breathlessly, her heart pounding. Held tightly against Matt's hard body, she was more aware of the strength of the arm holding her close than she was of Hob lying at their feet. The alarm on the face of the waitress and the interest of the only other customer didn't shake her euphoria. Against all odds, she had obtained what she had come for. She had done what needed to be done. The rest was in Matt's capable hands.

Matt turned to reassure the waitress as she hurried up. "Looks like Hob ran into a little trouble here," he said coolly. "But he'll be fine in a minute. Isn't that right, Hob?"

Hob muttered something indistinguishable and hitched himself up to a half-sitting position.

Matt turned away from the fallen man. All his cool impassiveness disappeared into a massive grin. "Let's get out of this place. I want to hear what's on that tape!"

The three of them crowded into the seat of Matt's truck, Jillian in the middle. Matt kept his arm around her while she rewound the tape and set the recorder on the dashboard to play.

Jillian found that the conversation between herself and Hob was almost as surprising to her as it was to the two men. She remembered very little of the actual words either of them had used. The sounds of the fight were muffled and indistinct, over almost as soon as they started.

No one said anything for a moment after the tape was finished.

"Play it again," Charley Alcott said.

They listened with rapt attention. Matt's arm tightened around Jillian. "You sure know how to talk!" he said admiringly. "Where did you learn all that legal jargon? 'Full disclosure,' and all the other stuff?"

Nestled comfortably against him, she smiled. "Oh, that. I used up my allotment of lies for this lifetime, I'm afraid. I didn't even know if I was making sense or not. I must have seen it on television. The same place that Hob Skinner learned that a private eye is supposed to carry a license."

As though the sound of his name had conjured him up, Hob pushed open the restaurant door and stepped out onto the sidewalk. Ignoring Matt's truck parked at the curb, he stalked away down the street.

"Doesn't look like you did him any damage, Matt," Charley Alcott commented as Hob climbed into his own battered pickup and drove off.

Jillian reached out to turn off the tape recorder. "What are you planning to do with this?" she asked tentatively.

The men exchanged glances. Charley Alcott shrugged. "Speaking personally, I'll take considerable satisfaction in listening to it a few dozen more times. Hob explaining that he didn't really 'plan' to do it and that it was 'practically an accident,' is more than I ever expected to hear."

Matt was a little uncertain, too. "I'm not sure where we ought to go from here," he said. "Hob was right—it isn't the kind of evidence that would stand up in court. I guess we just go back to business as usual. Only, from now on, if anybody starts to rake up the story about Charley's engine being at fault, we can just invite him out to listen to what Hob says on that tape."

Jillian felt a small twinge of disappointment through her euphoria. "It seems as though Hob is getting off too easily, without paying for what he did."

"The truth will get around," Matt said positively. "And things will be pretty uncomfortable for him around here."

"What do you think he'll do?" she asked.

"Well, I'm reasonably sure that he's not about to charge me with assault and battery." There was a smile in Matt's voice. "If ever a man needed to stay out of the spotlight, that's Hob right now. I don't think there's anything that he *can* do, except pack up his bank account and leave town."

"Let's us get out of here, too," Charley Alcott said. He opened the pickup door. "Suppose I meet you at your place, Matt. I'll bring the champagne for the celebration."

The two men were determined to drink to Jillian, but she was having none of that. "We did it together. None of us could have made it work without the other two."

They were sitting around the checkered tablecloth in the kitchen, drinking from stemmed glasses of fine crystal, mementos of bygone days of prosperity. Days that might yet come again, Jillian thought, now that Matt and his uncle were on friendly terms once more.

The tape recorder held the place of honor in the center of the table. Through a slight haze of champagne, Hob's words sounded even more damning than before, their own strategies even more brilliant.

Jillian gradually withdrew from the conversation. She sat twirling her glass gently by the stem, listening to the other two in a state of dreamy exhilaration. Everything was perfect now. No more worries, no more cares. Matt would keep his ranch; Charley could start up work in the logging camp again. They would both be paid handsomely by the motion picture company—the *movie*! She sat bolt upright. She had forgotten all about the movie. How could she have forgotten a thing like that? What was she doing here, sipping champagne in the middle of the afternoon, as though she didn't have a thing to do?

She put down her glass with a sudden movement and looked quickly around the room, then remembered that the telephone was in the living room. "I have to call Andrea," she said into a surprised silence. "I have to tell her that I'm on my way home."

* * *

Coming slowly back to the kitchen, Jillian was just about to push open the door when she heard Charley Alcott say, "You're a fool if you let that girl get away from you, Matt."

Jillian abhorred eavesdropping, but it wasn't humanly possible to tiptoe away from the answer to that statement.

"I've got some big problems to get straightened out around here first," Matt said.

"You don't have to worry about the bank anymore," his uncle said. "It'll be all right."

Jillian exhaled a breath she didn't even realize she had been holding. So now it was settled: in his taciturn way, Charley had just assured Matt of his financial backing.

"If she goes away today," the older man went on, "she won't have any reason to come back. Unless that movie really does get itself made in this vicinity. What are the chances of that?"

"I don't know," Matt said. "After today, I'm beginning to believe that anything's possible."

"It seems like a pretty long shot to me," Charley Alcott answered. "I wouldn't want to stake a whole lot on that happening. So you ought to figure that Jillian just might not be back this way again."

She waited for Matt's answer, her body tense.

"The road runs both ways. I can find my way to Portland without too much trouble." His voice changed, lightened. "Here, have the last of the champagne, Charley. We've celebrated all the way to the bottom of the bottle."

Jillian put out her hand to push open the door just as Charley spoke again.

"Wait a minute, Matt." Jillian waited, too. "If these movie people come here, they'll have their eye on my train and your ranch. So, between the two of us, we've got them whipsawed. Whatever we ask for, they'll have to give us. Within reason. And I don't see anything unreasonable in making it a condition that they hire Jillian to work on their movie. That would be a nice little something that you and I could do for her—show our appreciation for everything she's done for us.''

Jillian stood rigid, afraid to hear what was coming next.

"I think Jillian really wants that job." Matt's voice was quiet, thoughtful. "She said as much the first day she showed up here."

"That's settled, then." There was the sound of wooden chair legs being pushed back along the floor. "I'll just go tell her the good news."

Jillian beat a hasty tiptoed retreat back to the living room. She waited with her hands clenched, thinking incoherently that she had actually believed that Matt was different, that he understood how she felt, that he realized she could stand on her own two feet....

Seconds ticked away. Charley Alcott didn't appear at the other end of the hallway. Jillian took a deep breath, then exhaled slowly and made herself walk back to the kitchen.

Matt and his uncle were sitting at the table as she had left them. Aside from the fact that the champagne bottle was empty and Charley was looking a little tight-lipped, everything was the same as before.

Matt smiled at her, his eyes as innocent and guileless as a sunny sky. Apparently he had convinced Charley to save his announcement until the deed was accomplished. "What did Andrea have to say?" he asked.

"She says to get her car back to Portland on the double, she's going crazy taking taxis." Jillian reached for the strap to her bag. "I have to get going." She looked at Matt, disappointment clouding her eyes. "I guess this is goodbye."

Chapter Thirteen

Jillian sat between Matt and his uncle, trying to sort out her feelings as they drove into town. The two men talked over her head about cattle breeding and how soon Charley could hire a crew and start up his logging business again. Both of them were so careful to avoid mentioning the movie that she was miserably certain that it was as much on their minds as it was on hers.

If Matt truly believed that he'd be doing her a favor by forcing the production company to take her on, then he had a completely false picture of the kind of person she was. The situation was all the more maddening because she wasn't in a position to turn to him and tell him flatly that he wasn't to even *think* about doing such a thing. To do that, she'd have to confess to eavesdropping, which was just a shade less despicable than cramming an unwanted employee down an employer's throat as a condition of signing a business agreement.

Jillian wished passionately that she had never heard the tag end of their conversation. If only the telephone call had been a few seconds longer—or shorter—she never would have been seduced into listening at the door, she never would have known what they had in mind.

No, she contradicted herself unhappily, it was better this way. It was vitally important for her to understand exactly how Matt saw her, how he felt about her work, her attitude toward self-reliance. Better to know that he felt them unimportant enough that he could conspire to hand her a prized job like an adult capturing a pretty balloon for a helpless toddler.

How could Matt do a thing like that, say such things, feel that way about her? Every time she let down her guard, allowed herself to believe that he was able to see her as a human being and not a Dresden doll, that forceful Western maleness of his broke through again. Sometimes it almost seemed that she was the one at fault, always insisting on having what no one else was willing to give, wanting to be an equal partner, not a pampered house pet.

She felt an aching hollow inside her as she looked down a long future that didn't include Matt. It's better this way, she told herself again, better to know now. But a desolate loneliness inside of her threatened to turn into a flood of scalding tears, and it took all her strength to hold them back.

At the motel, Matt stowed her overnight case in the Porsche and then ducked his head down to speak to her through the driver's window.

"I'll see you in Portland in a couple of days," he said.

She took a long last look at those farseeing blue eyes, and the thick fair hair that needed cutting.

"You don't even know where I live," she pointed out a little more sharply than she intended.

"But I have your telephone number, right here on your business card." He patted his shirt pocket and gave her a confident grin. "You can give me directions when I call you tomorrow."

"I may be hard to locate," Jillian said. "Andrea will have so much work lined up for me that I'll need to be twins. And, anyway—" she paused briefly "—you ought to stay put until we get the final verdict from the people in Los Angeles."

He shook his head. "That could take weeks," he protested.

"Sometimes they move faster than you'd believe possible," she said. "If the producer likes the snapshots, he may say This Is It! and someone from his staff could be on your doorstep by the day after tomorrow. They'll want to talk to you, so you'd better be here."

"We'll see." Matt didn't sound convinced. He cocked an eye at her. "Maybe you think I should spruce the place up? Buy some lace curtains, or something?"

"Don't you dare. It's—it's just right the way it is." Jillian's voice was threatening to break. She quickly turned the ignition key and put the car in gear. She backed out and left him standing there waving goodbye so cheerfully because he expected to see her again very soon.

Jillian was busy when Matt called her. That seemed reasonable at first, he was pretty busy himself. But each time he insisted on making the trip to Portland, she put him off, insisting that he wait at the ranch for the men from Los Angeles to show up. They were definitely coming, she was sure of it, tomorrow or the next day or the day after that. And finally they actually did come, and the deal was approved and the contracts signed with handshakes all around. And when Matt called to say he was on his way to the city to celebrate with her, Jillian was sorry but she was just leaving for a small town in southern Oregon where she was going to be terribly busy again preparing to shoot a bank commercial that Andrea had lined up.

Something was definitely wrong, but Matt couldn't figure out what. And it looked as though he would have to track her all over the state to find out what was going on. He had made up his mind to do just that when he walked out of the barn one afternoon to see the little red Porsche speeding up the road to the house. He couldn't believe his good fortune.

He hurried to the spot where the car pulled up in front of the house. A tall, fashionably dressed brunette slid out of the driver's seat and extended her hand to him.

"You must be Matt," she said as he looked past her into the empty car. "I'm Andrea DiCicco. I'm here in Enterprise with a couple of Bernie's aides, and I thought I'd steal a few minutes to meet you and see the famous ranch that Jillian's talked so much about."

"Come inside and have coffee." Matt tried to cover his disappointment with politeness. "Is Jillian with you?" he asked, not very hopefully.

"Not this trip. We're here to introduce ourselves to the local bigwigs. She'll arrive the first of the week with some of the others to get started on the basics—arranging for rooms and transportation and a few thousand things like that."

"Come in for coffee," he said again, suddenly eager to prolong the conversation.

"Thanks, but I can't this time. I'm due back ten minutes ago." She surveyed the buildings and surroundings with a long appreciative look that reminded him poignantly of Jillian's first arrival—that was just the way she had stood, had looked around. . . .

"It's going to be perfect," Andrea said. "The biggest thing DiCicco Productions has ever done. Everything's working out beautifully. Although I suppose I'll be looking for a new production assistant when this is over," she said as she turned away to slide into the car.

Matt couldn't have agreed more, but he was surprised that she should refer to it, that his intentions had been so obvious. Strange, too, that Jillian would have said anything to Andrea, after the unresolved way things had been left between them. And after the way she'd been acting for nearly two weeks now, almost as though she'd been dodging him.

"You think you'll be looking for someone to fill Jillian's job?"

"That's right. Bernie's company will be using her for the duration of the shoot." Andrea settled herself behind the wheel. "And she's such a dynamite worker, I bet she'll be California-bound by the time the summer is over."

Matt stepped back. He watched her go, his jaw clenched. He immediately attempted to reach Jillian, but only got in touch again with her telephone recorder and its business-like repetition of the same old statement: she was out of town, but if he would like to leave a message...

Matt was in no mood for leaving messages. Only the knowledge that she was scheduled to be in Enterprise very soon kept him from jumping in the truck and heading for Portland. But there was no sense in knocking on the door of an empty apartment, maybe passing her on the road when she was going in the opposite direction. In her own territory she could avoid him—if that's what she was doing—but she wasn't going to get away with that once she was back on his stamping grounds.

Because he was fired up and had to do *something*, he drove into town and confirmed that Jillian had a reservation for Monday at the Wilderness Inn.

It was late in the afternoon when Jillian eased her old Volkswagen van into the parking lot behind the motel. Coming back had been harder than she had expected. Memories made her heart turn over without warning. She should have been strong enough to refuse the job that had been handed her. Now she would never know if they would have wanted her for herself if she hadn't been forced on them. It had been a hard struggle this past week, a wrenching decision between refusing the job or taking it on and doing it so well that she'd show all of them that she was the best choice for it...no matter why they had hired her.

With uncharacteristic slowness, she pushed open the door and stepped out—and turned to find Matt striding toward her with a grim expression on his face.

"What—what are you doing here?" It wasn't fair; she wasn't ready for this. Not ready for the impact of his presence, for the desolation that filled her heart at the fresh realization of what might have been.

"I'm taking you to dinner," Matt said.

"I can't," she said quickly. "I'm with some of the movie people. I'm supposed to show them—"

"They'll find a restaurant without your help." His voice was quiet but filled with a hard certainty that allowed for no argument.

His eyes held hers with an intensity that made her feel an unfamiliar weakness. Though her mind held back, her body ached to go with him. She trembled inwardly at the touch of his hand on her arm, the strong hard hand that was turning her, guiding her to his familiar old pickup truck. She squeezed her eyes shut briefly, as though trying to disentangle herself from an alluring spell, but she heeded the little voice inside her that urged her to go along, to go with him now. It had to be done sometime, and putting it off wouldn't make it any easier.

"Where are you going?" she whispered when the truck turned away from town.

"Willy stuck a roast in the oven and took off," he said. "We're going to have a little privacy to talk."

Not fair, she thought. She had expected a restaurant; polite controlled voices in an impersonal atmosphere. A place where she could explain quietly and rationally that each of them had misjudged the other.

A vehicle was already parked in front of the ranch house. As they drew up beside it, Jillian recognized Charley Alcott's truck. Matt got out, swearing under his breath.

The door opened as they approached. The smell of good food cooking wafted toward them. "I expected you before this," his uncle greeted them.

"What are you doing here?" Matt demanded ungraciously.

"I talked to Willy. He said Jillian was coming, so I stopped by." Charley Alcott seemed oblivious of the tension between them. "I brought Jillian a little something as a token of appreciation for all she did for us," he said, ushering them inside.

"No. You shouldn't have." Jillian made a little gesture of protest.

Charley Alcott took no notice. He produced a small flat velvet jeweler's box and held it out to her.

Jillian made no move to accept. Hadn't they done enough already? she thought despairingly.

"It's not much," he said, "just a little keepsake to remember us by." He opened the box so she could see a small old-fashioned cameo, a woman's profile, exquisitely carved, set in a circlet of antique gold filigree, on a fine gold chain.

"It was my mother's," Charley Alcott said. "Matt's grandmother. I thought you might like it."

"It's lovely." Jillian's voice was strained. "But I really don't think that I should—"

"Go ahead," he urged her. "If it wasn't for this ungrateful whelp here, we would have come up with a lot more substantial token of our esteem, but he wouldn't have it—"

"Never mind about that, Charley," Matt said warningly.

Jillian looked from one to the other. "I don't understand."

Charley Alcott said, "I was all for making those movie people write you into the contracts, just to make sure you got that job you were hoping for, but Matt wouldn't have any part of it. He wouldn't even let me bring it up to them. But I guess it turned out all right—here you are back again."

"Yes, here I am," she said, a little dizzy with surprise and sudden happiness. She held out her hand, and Charley placed the little velvet box in it. "Thank you," she said. "I-I'll treasure this. It's an heirloom."

"Well, good." Charley Alcott surveyed the two of them with pleasure. "I don't guess I'll hang around for dinner," he said with elephantine tact. "I'll just be on my way," he added when no one pressed him to stay.

Once they were alone, Jillian looked down at the cameo in her hand, then at Matt and at the big masculine room.

"Something's changed," Matt said. "You're smiling."

She could feel that she was, indeed, smiling through happy tears. She blinked them back and stretched out her arms to him.

His embrace was like coming home at last, with burdens lifted, clouds dispersed. Their bodies molded together as though they were one person, with no boundaries or self to set them apart.

Jillian raised a blissful—and guilty—face to his. "I have a confession to make," she told him bravely.

His strong arms tightened around her. He led her to the big leather sofa and pulled her down beside him. "What dark crimes have you committed now?" he asked indulgently.

Jillian could feel a blush warming her skin. "I listened at the door," she forced herself to say. She told him about hearing Charley's plan to get her the job and then hurrying away when he got up to come and tell her about it. "I thought you agreed with him. I was so disappointed."

Matt laid his cheek against her hair. "Too bad you didn't stay to hear the finish. After all, Charley sat down and shut up. Why did you think he did that?"

"I guessed that you convinced him to keep it as a surprise. Or—" her voice dropped a little lower "—maybe you weren't going to tell me at all. Just let me go on believing I got the job all on my own, like a grown-up woman."

His hands caressed her back, spanned her waist, pulled her to him fiercely. "You're all the woman any man could want. And don't you forget it." Holding her close, he added, "I have a confession to make, too."

She waited, not knowing what to expect.

"I love you."

She tilted her head up to look at him. "That doesn't sound so terrible to me," she said, smiling.

"You haven't heard the terrible part yet. I love you so much that I don't want you to go away to Hollywood and have a great career and become rich and famous. I'm rotten enough to wish you would give all that up and stay here with me."

"Oh, Matt," she said fondly. "I never was on the road to being rich and famous, only to having a job that I can do well, that was all."

"If it's a *job* you're looking for—" his eyes lighted up "—I happen to know of an executive position right here, and it's one that no one but you could possibly fill."

"And what would the job description be?" Jillian asked, suddenly breathless.

"Sweetheart," he said. "Lover. Partner. Wife."

In answer, she raised her lips to meet his.

Many minutes later, he said, "Is that a yes?"

She nodded. "Absolutely."

He uncoiled like a steel spring, rising to his feet, sweeping her up in his arms, stamping around the room with a yell of delight.

Jillian clung to him, laughing, sharing his elation.

"How long does it take to get married?" he demanded. "A week?"

"If only we could," she said. "Even I can't even organize a movie with one hand and a wedding with the other. Besides," she added saucily, coaxing the shadow of disappointment from his eyes, "If we wait until the film wraps, you'll have more time to find out what it's like to have a managing woman in your life."

He whirled her around again. "Well, anyway, here's a preview of coming attractions!" His lips found hers once more.

The sweet fire of love coursed through her veins, turning all her precious practicality into dreamy languor. It seemed an eternity before the outside world became real again. The rich aroma of the roast in the oven finally penetrated her senses, and Jillian wondered, still dreamily, what chance she'd have of not burning the gravy *this* time.

*   *   *   *   *

You'll flip . . . your pages won't!
Read paperbacks *hands-free* with

Book Mate • I

The perfect "mate" for all your romance paperbacks

Traveling • Vacationing • At Work • In Bed • Studying • Cooking • Eating

Perfect size for all standard paperbacks, this wonderful invention makes reading a pure pleasure! Ingenious design holds paperback books OPEN and FLAT so even wind can't ruffle pages — leaves your hands free to do other things. Reinforced, wipe-clean vinyl-covered holder flexes to let you turn pages without undoing the strap . . . supports paperbacks so well, they have the strength of hardcovers!

Pages turn WITHOUT opening the strap.

SEE-THROUGH STRAP

Reinforced back stays flat.

Built in bookmark.

BOOK MARK

BACK COVER HOLDING STRIP

10" x 7¼", opened.
Snaps closed for easy carrying, too.

Available now. Send your name, address, and zip code, along with a check or money order for just $5.95 + .75¢ for postage & handling (for a total of $6.70) payable to Reader Service to:

Reader Service
Bookmate Offer
901 Fuhrmann Blvd.
P.O. Box 1396
Buffalo, N.Y. 14269-1396

Offer not available in Canada
*New York and Iowa residents add appropriate sales tax.

BM-G

FOUR UNIQUE SERIES
FOR EVERY WOMAN YOU ARE...

Silhouette Romance

Love, at its most tender, provocative, emotional... in stories that will make you laugh and cry while bringing you the magic of falling in love.

6 titles per month

Silhouette Special Edition

Sophisticated, substantial and packed with emotion, these powerful novels of life and love will capture your imagination and steal your heart.

6 titles per month

Silhouette Desire

Open the door to romance and passion. Humorous, emotional, compelling—yet always a believable and sensuous story—Silhouette Desire never fails to deliver on the promise of love.

6 titles per month

Silhouette Intimate Moments

Enter a world of excitement, of romance heightened by suspense, adventure and the passions every woman dreams of. Let us sweep you away.

4 titles per month

SILG-1R

COMING NEXT MONTH

#652 THE ENCHANTED SUMMER—Victoria Glenn
When Derek Randall was sent to Green Meadow to buy the rights to
the "Baby Katy" doll, he found himself more interested in rights
holder Katy Kruger—a real live doll herself!

#653 AGELESS PASSION, TIMELESS LOVE—
Phyllis Halldorson
CEO Courtney Forrester had always discouraged office romances at
his plant. But Assistant Personnel Manager Kirsten Anderson was
proof that rules were meant to be broken....

#654 HIS KIND OF WOMAN—Pat Tracy
As the widow of his boyhood rival, Grace Banner was certainly not
Matthew Hollister's kind of woman...until a passionate battle led
Matthew to a tender change of heart.

#655 TREASURE HUNTERS—Val Whisenand
When Lori Kendall became a contestant on a TV game show she
discovered that the only prize worth winning was teammate Jason
Daniels. But would Jason's secret send Lori home empty-handed?

#656 IT TAKES TWO—Joan Smith
As concierge of an upscale Montreal hotel, Jennie Longman was used
to catering to her guests' eccentric whims. But Wes Adler had a
request that wasn't in Jennie's handbook. He wanted her!

#657 TEACH ME—Stella Bagwell
When secretary Bernadette Baxter started teaching her boss, Nicholas
Atwood, the fine art of dating, she was soon wishing she was the
woman who'd reap the benefits of her lessons....

AVAILABLE THIS MONTH